THE VAMPIRE'S ESCAPE

A PARANORMAL ROMANCE

AJ TIPTON

Please, *let tonight be the night*, Lauren prayed into the gold-lined bathroom mirror as she dabbed a smudge of lipstick off of her teeth. The dress she was wearing was the same one she wore on her previous date with Trevor, but she'd convinced a seamstress friend to take it apart and make it look new. She winced as a hastily-sewn seam dug into her back. All the expenses and favors to keep up appearances were piling up, and if Trevor didn't come through, she was screwed. *Trevor has to be the one.*

Lauren forced herself not to focus on the lines that had recently appeared around her eyes and mouth. Thirty-eight had not been as kind as thirty-five, and the last three years since Nikolai had died had taken a toll she couldn't afford to show on her face. She padded on some more concealer. It wouldn't do if hot, billionaire Trevor Simm realized she wasn't the twenty-seven-year-old she'd claimed to be.

She adjusted her breasts a little higher into the swooping neckline of her dress, then pushed them down an inch. The trick was to pull off that delicate balance between "lady" and "fuckable", riding both identities convincingly. It made a man recognize he had to *earn* his place in her bed, but also feel confident he would get there eventually. After six months of Trevor's studious and attentive courtship, tonight *had* to be night he'd trade a ring for the honor of having Lauren as his companion for the rest of his life.

You can do this, she told her reflection. *This is what you've trained for your whole life.* Lauren smiled at herself, a well-practiced smile both winning and polite that didn't show teeth--*A lady does not grimace like a chimpanzee*, her mother's words chided in her head—as she soldiered back out into the restaurant.

Chez Fenêtre was still as beautiful as it had been years ago when she was a regular every Tuesday night with Nikolai. Lauren had gently led Trevor into coming up with the idea of inviting her here for their six-month anniversary, calling ahead so the host and staff would know to pretend not to recognize her, but also have her favorite red wine in stock.

Trevor stood as she approached, polite as always, with a tiny, no-teeth smile that Lauren's mother would approve of completely. Detached and charming, like Clark Gable in a black-and-white noir, but with blond hair slicked to the side like a Ken doll, and a slight build. Although he claimed he was thirty, he looked twenty-two at the most.

And Trevor had *money*.

So much money. The kind of money that wore bespoke suits and hand-crafted watches, drove a different Aston Martin every time he picked her up, and flew her on a private jet to Paris for dinner dates.

Her late husband, Nikolai, had been extremely well off, the retired Alpha of a bear shifter clan worth several billion dollars. They'd married as an explicit business arrangement: she provided him companionship and care in return for Nikolai sharing the extravagance of his extremely comfortable lifestyle. Although neither had ever claimed to love the other, over the fifteen years they were together, they developed a real fondness. Every day, Lauren missed the small kindnesses they'd exchanged even to Nikolai's last moments, and the comfort of knowing that she never had to take care of anything except Nikolai's immediate needs.

But when the cancer finally took him, she'd discovered Nikolai's wealth had been his son's all along. The young Alpha granted Lauren a modest stipend to carry her through until she figured out how to support herself, but the money always disappeared faster than she planned.

Trevor pulled out Lauren's chair and motioned for her to sit down. The waiter was gone, their meal already cleared, but two glasses of champagne stood on the table, with another bottle waiting for them in a silver ice bucket. Her heartbeat quickened.

This is it!

"You look lovely tonight, my dear." Trevor's speech was always a little stilted. But it was all part of his odd charm. He had an old-fashioned nature layered with awkwardness that was cute and endearing, very different from Nikolai's rough confidence.

She smiled, thanking him with an upward glance through her eyebrows to check if his eyes were--*yes, they are*--fixed on her face rather than her breasts. No amount of money would be worth the pawing she got from a few of the men she'd dated soon after Nikolai's passing. Trevor had stood out immediately from the crowd when he never pushed to get physical, agreeing with her insistence that they wait until they were fully committed. The furthest they'd gone was the passionate kissing they'd exchanged on the flight back from their last diving date in the Red Sea.

Trevor had been a great kisser, employing just the right

amount of tongue, his hands skimming her breasts with enough delicacy to make her nipples tighten, but avoided being grabby. Even if she'd never mistake it for love, remembering his lips' confident path down her neck and along her chest widened the smile she beamed across the table.

"I'm so happy, Trevor," she said. "Thank you so much for another beautiful night." She indicated the empty, luxurious restaurant around them. He'd bought out the entire place so they could have privacy; only their waiter and the kitchen staff were present, however professionally invisible, during their four-course meal. "I've never been as happy as when I'm with you."

A lie. But it wasn't Trevor's fault she didn't love him yet. He was respectful and sweet. She'd love him eventually.

Trevor smiled. "I am so pleased to hear you say that." He stood up from his chair, took one of the glasses of champagne off of the table, and got down on one knee in front of her.

Yes, yes, yes, yes. Lauren pressed her hands together to keep from clapping in wild glee. *I did it! I did it! At thirty-eight, I still got it!*

"Lauren Vaughan." He slid out a long box from his pocket, far too large for a ring, and flipped it open.

What? She stared at the knife inside the box. It was heavily bejeweled, including a diamond as big as a walnut, the blade only about an inch long, and wickedly sharp.

"Um," she started to say, then stopped. *It's a tiny knife. Let's see how this goes.* But, with her feet hidden under the table's draping tablecloth, she slipped out of her heels, ready to run if the situation called for it.

Trevor smiled at her and pricked the top of his ring finger with the knife, dripping the blood into his champagne. The bubbling liquid turned slowly crimson as the blood mixed with the golden fizz.

"Will you, my love, be my eternal bride of the night?" He raised the glass toward her.

Vampire. It explained so much. His old-fashioned language, how he had so much money without having any sign of an inheritance or job, and his face looked far too young for how he acted. She bit her lip, keeping her face curious as she rapidly thought it through.

Nikolai told her about vampires as part of her introduction to the supernatural world when they were first getting to know each other. She'd never really considered finding someone to turn her--if she had, she'd have done it before the most recent set of wrinkles set in--but why not? She wasn't getting any younger, and Trevor was everything she'd ever looked for in a life companion: rich, kind, and malleable.

"I don't understand. What are you saying?" *Rule one of being a lady: never let a man know what you know.* As far as Trevor was concerned, Lauren was completely oblivious to the supernatural world. She took the glass of red-tinted champagne from his hand and placed it on the table in front of her. He smiled at the gesture and settled back in the chair opposite her.

"I am a vampire, my sweet, just like that masterful character of legend, Dracula. It may be difficult to believe, but witches, werewolves and many other magical beings are all real. *I* am real." He opened his lips and flashed his teeth at her. Even expecting them, Lauren was startled to see his canines elongate down from his mouth until they pressed deep into his lower lip.

"You're a *vampire*?" She made her voice rise in a high note of incredulousness. "You drink *blood*?"

He smiled, that same aloof smirk. "Indeed, I need blood to survive, but I also enjoy the fine foods and lovely meals we've shared. Never fear, I procure my blood from donors. You are safe from my hunger."

She nodded, his answer lining up with what she already knew.

"But, we've been out in the sun together. I thought vampires couldn't go outside during the day." She questioned him, only half listening to his responses, tallying up the answers she knew to be true, playing the part of the ignorant human to give Trevor the opportunity to lie.

"Indeed, we are weakened during the day," he said. "Our strength and senses are more limited, and direct sunlight can be painful, but I am able to walk in the light."

All true, she nodded to herself. It would have been easy for Trevor to lie about the negative side of vampiric life, but-- even though it was clear he wanted Lauren to join him--he didn't.

"That's a relief."

If Trevor was surprised that she was believing him so fast, he certainly didn't show it. Lauren catalogued all the pros and cons Nikolai had told her about vampires: super strength and enhanced senses would be nice (although she wasn't sure when she'd have occasion to use them), and she'd be able to smell the emotions in non-vampires (also, not that useful). Never enjoying the feel of the sun against her skin would be disappointing, but she rarely braved skin-damaging UV rays these days anyway.

She touched her cheek. *I'll never be worried about wrinkles again!* It would be definitely worth it to stop aging, to heal quickly, and to be ultimately invincible to anything but fire or beheading...but then there was the *hortari*. She eyed Trevor. She'd spent the last six months evaluating him as a husband, but as a sire?

Vampire sires had total command over their sirelings' actions; if he chose to employ the hortari, Trevor's will would supersede her own. *That shouldn't be too bad*, she thought, biting the inside of her cheek. In their six months of courtship, he had never raised his voice to her, and been consistently courteous and generous.

"If you turn me into a vampire, what will that mean for *us*?" She worded her question as vaguely as possible, studying his face for any hint that he knew she was dissembling.

He smiled, reaching out across the table to settle his hand on top of hers. "Since our first glance, I knew you were the one who should spend eternity my side. If I turn you into a vampire, I will be your sire, which means I will have the power of *hortari* over you." Lauren relaxed as soon as he said the word. Trevor brought up the *hortari* when he could easily have lied about it.

"With the *hortari*, I will have the ability to control you with my words, if I choose." Trevor paused, his fingers caressing the top of her hand. "But the *hortari* is only meant to be used in moments of desperate need, to keep new vampires from hurting others as they adjust to their hunger and new abilities. I love you so much, Lauren, I would never command you to do anything you didn't want to."

Lauren's heart soared. He *was* a good man. A good vampire. She'd chosen well. *And I'm going to live forever!* Forever secure. Forever protected. Never having to worry about hiding another wrinkle, or being dumped for someone younger. No more depending on the generosity of her stepson who had never really gotten over the fifty year age difference between her and Nikolai.

She reached across the table to brush her hand along the side of Trevor's face. He was so handsome, he was like an airbrushed movie poster come to life. And he wanted *her*. Thirty-eight year-old, widowed Lauren Vaughan.

"Yes," she said. "I will be your--" *What was that ridiculous way he'd phrased it?* --"bride of the night."

"You breathtaking creature." He threw his head back, his voice deepening. "There are darknesses in life and there are lights, and you are one of the lights, the light of all lights."

Faster even than Nikolai, with all his bear-shifter speed, had ever moved, Trevor tossed the table so it tumbled away from them, champagne and glassware smashing against the opposite wall.

Trevor moved so quickly, Lauren didn't even see him get up, but his hands were on either side of her face and his mouth was on hers, pressing hard with devouring strokes of his tongue. Months of pent-up passion and lust for his hard-cut body flared to life and she pulled him closer until they spilled off of her chair and onto the restaurant's lush carpeting.

His need for her pulled at longings she'd been pushing down for years. He ripped off her dress and Lauren was grateful she'd gone with her sexiest bra and no panties. Trevor's eyes roamed her body and she raised her arms above her head, lifting her breasts up and toward him. She knew she looked hot. She'd worked *hard* to stay this hot. She ran four miles a day, hadn't eaten a carb in ten years, and forced down kale even though it tasted like sour dirt. But it was all worth it for the look in Trevor's eyes.

The man practically drooled at the sight of her, and she squirmed with delight. He tore off his shirt, displaying all the muscles that his perfectly-tailored suits had always hinted lay hidden beneath his posh exterior.

The desperate hunger on his face made arousal pool between Lauren's legs. It had been a *long* three years. She grabbed Trevor's hands, pressing his fingers to her clit as she ravaged his lips. Her hips bucked against his hand, driving her pleasure as the weight of his body pressed on top of hers, building delicious friction against her most sensitive places. She unbuckled his belt, tossing it away. He didn't wait for her to undo the rest of his pants, he simply tore apart the fabric down to his boxers so his erect cock sprang free.

Trevor stroked his cock as his other hand sped up against her clit to a supernatural speed that almost felt like her trusty vibrator at home. Lauren purred at the sensation, kissing his neck and unhooking her bra so she could rub her pointed nipples against his bare chest. His skin was cold, a relief from the warmth building up from between her legs. It was all so fast, she needed his *want*, needed him to not take back his offer of eternal security.

Lauren rolled them over so she was on top, facing away from Trevor. She leaned forward and kissed a trail down Trevor's abs to where she wanted to be. Her lips fastened around his cock, licking up and down his shaft, then kissing downward to take his balls one at a time between her lips as her fingers lavished attention along his dick. He groaned and she pressed Trevor's fingers deeper inside herself so she could fuck his fingers as she licked his cock.

"Oh baby, you're so hot." Trevor groaned. "Your mouth...your fucking mouth." Lauren smiled, power flowing through her like a drug, thrilling at how she broke through Trevor's old-fashioned speech to make him totally lose control. He was always so aloof, his look of helpless abandon as he grabbed the back of her head and fucked her mouth in earnest sent a thrill down to her toes.

He pulled out from her lips at the last moment. "Gods, baby, I need you." He gently pushed her onto her back and she spread open for him, the sweat dripping down his face the highest compliment she'd gotten in ages.

"Come inside me, Trevor." Lauren ground her hips up against his cock, her legs spreading to hook behind his back, pressing her wet core against his tip. "Please, I need more."

"Oh baby, you can have more. You can have everything." He surged deep into her, fucking her fast and hard. She swung her hips up to meet every stroke, her fingers slipping in-between their bodies to finger her clit as his cock pulled out an inch to thrust back in.

He pounded her over and over, words of "harder" and "faster" and "fuck, yes!" intermingling with each other and then degrading into animal grunts and screams as Trevor's cock moved inside of her. Pleasure built like a surging wave with each touch to her clit until he came inside her, and she followed him over the edge. Just as the orgasm started to subside, Trevor's wrist pressed against her lips and a metallic, salty liquid touched her tongue. She looked up into his eyes, his breathing fast, each exhale of his chest brushing against her nipples.

"Drink, my love. Drink and be mine."

She opened her mouth and sucked on the blood, feeling it roll down her throat. A heavy, languid feeling settled over her and Lauren closed her eyes.

Vampirism, here I come.

THE SUN SET behind Trevor's mansion, blocking the last rays peeking through the blinds of Ben's lab. The small house, set up in the back of Trevor's enormous property behind the pool, was Ben's domain, although it was not without its perils. A dangerous, hiccupping sound came from the table nearest the window, and Ben dove for cover.

His latest invention gurgled like a kangaroo giving birth and whipped around in circles, spurting out liquid before letting out a sad puff of smoke. Ben peeked out from his protective stack of toolboxes and stroked his chin, surprised at the short beard he found. *Didn't I just shave this morning?* He wondered. A glance at his phone. Four days ago. It had been days since he shaved. Or fed.

He scrawled a note in his lab journal and grabbed a bag of blood from the mini-fridge, grateful his nephew, Trevor, remembered to keep it stocked. The blood was donated by an old horse shifter after a day at the spa and tasted of her calm. He let the blood slide smoothly down his throat, and approached his malfunctioning invention with healthy caution.

The gurgling pipes and spinning gears seemed to be in good order, just coated with gas. "Blast and tarnation," Ben cursed. He picked up a rag and gently stroked the sides, wiping off the machine's unfortunate byproduct. The drained blood bag dropped forgotten to his feet.

Ben's latest invention was going to be a game-changer for humanity, if he could just stop it from spraying gasoline everywhere. The desalinator functioned as a component conversion device, turning plastic waste and saltwater into fresh, drinkable water. The only byproduct was gasoline, which Ben couldn't seem to get rid of.

"Hello? Dude?" An unfamiliar voice called out.

"Coming!" Ben wound his way through his lab, turning and inching sideways so his wide shoulders wouldn't topple any of the precarious stacks lining the path down the center of the room. Ben's piles of lab journals, books, beakers, and tools appeared as disorganized chaos to the uneducated eye, but to Ben, his lab's functional disorder was one of his finest feats of engineering.

A gawky human teenager stood just outside the pool house's wide, glass doors. Ben's vampiric nose could smell the teen's boredom and impatience emanating from the boy's blood.

"Pizza delivery." The pizza boy grunted. He shifted his weight, straining under the weight of the seven pizzas stacked almost to his chin.

Ben furrowed his brow. "I didn't order... Nobody here really...*eats*, you see."

From the delivery boy's puzzled expression, it was clear that he did *not* see.

Right. Human. Ben slapped the side of his head, and the boy jumped a little.

"Oops...," Ben chuckled, hoping to set the poor kid at ease. "What I mean is, *of course* we eat. We humans love eating the foods. It's just that..." Ben tried to lean casually on a nearby lab table, and ended up planting his palm in a petri dish of sky worms. He peeled the sticky worms off his hand and deposited them back with their wiggling brothers. The teenager's eyes followed the worms from Ben's hand and back to the dish and he paled.

Ben scooped up a large wrench and began to twirl it between his fingers, but the boy's expression didn't ease.

"Uh, dude? The order said to bring it to the pool house. This *is* the pool house, right?" The teenager resettled the boxes in his arms.

Oh, dear. I'm doing it again. Ben always got a bit flustered when interacting with strangers. He tended to over-articulate, flailing his arms wildly to better ensure he was understood. Once, Ben nearly took a gardener's eye out when chatting about desalination.

"Yes!" Ben cried. "This is my lab, which is situated next to my nephew, Trevor's, pool, which makes it the pool house. Do you see that lovely gothic mansion up the way? That's where he lives with his girlfriend."

The pizza boy had begun to back away slowly from the furious twirling of Ben's wrench. "Cool, dude...cool." He straightened up, suddenly business. "Well you gotta pay for these, man. My boss'll take it out of my check if you don't."

Ben dropped the wrench with a clatter. "Oh, certainly, of course." He patted down his pockets and pulled out a screwdriver and a handful of bolts. He chuckled uncomfortably. "I'm not great with currency." He rummaged around a cabinet under his lab table, pulling out a rusty coffee can. "I'm sure I have something in here." Ben coughed in the dust as he removed the plastic lid and poured out a fistful of paper and stones. He held it out to the teenager.

"That's like a thousand bucks, and I don't even know how much in..." The delivery boy juggled the stack of boxes slightly to get a closer look. "Are those emeralds?"

"A few emeralds, a ruby or two, and some pirate gold." Ben sighed. "Good times."

"Yeah, man, you owe me $83.95. I don't exactly have change for pirate gold."

"Of course." Ben thought hard for a moment. "Could I ask you to...? Would you be able to just keep all of it, then? That would be very convenient. I could get back to my work and you can use it to buy..." He ventured a guess. "A telescope or whatever you youths are into." He nodded, increasingly pleased at the idea. "Yes. That should work nicely."

"Wow, thanks, man. You're weird, but you're like, *super* nice." The pizza boy grinned and stuffed the lot into his pocket. "Where should I put these?" He nodded at the stack of pizzas.

"Right here." A radiant woman emerged from around the corner of the pool house. *Was she waiting back there?* Ben wondered.

The woman casually tossed her long, blonde hair over one shoulder. She was dressed in a nice dress and pearls that looked a little odd next to Ben's science equipment. In a single motion, she took the seven pizzas out of the delivery boy's arms with ease, holding the heavy stack in one perfectly-manicured hand.

"Bye!" The pizza boy disappeared, running across the wide lawn of Trevor's estate.

"Hello...Susan?" Ben ventured a guess. He thought that was Trevor's girlfriend's name, but hadn't her eyes been a paler blue? This woman's eyes were the dark blue of storms and indigo.

She tucked into the pizza without ceremony, holding the pile of boxes with one hand and the slice in the other while still standing in his doorway. She quickly destroyed the slice topped with bacon and avocado before turning to the other side of the pizza.

"Lauren," she said through a mouthful of food. "We actually haven't met."

"Oh, good. I'm Ben, Benjamin Dal." Ben cleared off two folding chairs, pushing one toward her before slumping into the other. "It's so much easier to meet somebody for the first time. I'm much less likely to have forgotten them."

Lauren nodded thanks for the chair, sitting down gingerly as she took out another slice. "You make a good point." She bit into the pizza and let out a low moan. Ben's eyes widened at the sound.

"So, Lauren." Ben drummed on his knees awkwardly. "What...I mean is, well, I don't want to be rude." He focused his gaze on a drop of grease which dropped from her pizza onto the ground. "Why are you eating pizza in my lab?" Trevor always had a girl-friend: blonde, tall, and lean vampires like Lauren. But they never came out to the pool house. He'd see them around the grounds, sometimes he'd hear them swimming at night, and then they'd leave. And a new one would show up a few months later. It made Ben a little uneasy that Trevor's girlfriends were also his sirelings--it could certainly make romance more complicated--but such relationships weren't *unheard* of.

"Trevor won't let me eat human food in the house." Lauren said it so matter-of-factly, for a second Ben wasn't sure he'd heard right. *Surely not.* Trevor wasn't letting her eat? That didn't sound reasonable at all.

She smiled and held out the rectangular cardboard box to Ben. "I didn't even know anyone lived out here. I thought the pool house was just filled with junk." Lauren ripped the top off of the box and created a makeshift plate for him, selecting a slice topped with maple bacon and jalapenos. "Give this a try. I bet they didn't make food like this back whenever you were turned."

Ben brought the slice to his lips and took a conservative bite. "I've never really been much of a food person--" He stopped short, the symphony of flavor overwhelming his palate. The taste was like a calm bonfire and a raucous fireworks display all at once. "My, this is delightful!" He chomped down another bite with gusto.

Lauren laughed, a melodic chorus that bubbled out of her, unrestrained. "Oh, we're just getting started. I am dubbing you my new secret pizza buddy." She brought her slice to his, knocking them together. "Clink. Pizza toast."

Ben chewed thoughtfully. "*Secret* pizza buddy, eh?"

Lauren rolled her eyes. "Trevor says since I'm so new to being a vampire, I should push away from my old human ways. As if I could have eaten like this while I was human. He's on a strict, all-blood diet, and thinks I should be, too."

"Surely you're having *some* blood?" Ben asked. Trevor was the sireling of Ben's brother, Danny, and had always been a little strange. But even if Ben's nephew had some weird ideas about how to teach new vampires about their new lives, surely he wasn't *starving* her.

"Of course!" she said and Ben relaxed a little. "But..." She gestured at her lean figure. "I worked my entire life to look a certain way, and that meant saying 'no' to food like this." Lauren grinned madly as she tore into a pepperoni slice.

"Now that these calories don't count, I'm sure as shit going to enjoy it."

"Is that why you became a vampire? Caloric freedom?" Ben held out his makeshift plate, and Lauren slid him another slice.

"That certainly didn't hurt. Neither did the immortality." Lauren laughed. "Can you keep a secret?"

Ben shrugged, pointing around his jumble of a lab. "Who's there to tell?"

Her lips quirked. "Trevor doesn't know I knew all about vampires before we met. My late husband was a bear shifter and he taught me a lot." She brought a finger to her lips. "Don't tell."

"*Late* husband? I'm so sorry." Ben leaned forward to touch her shoulder and she nodded. "You must miss him."

"I'm not even sure why I'm telling you, but I've been living here for a month now and sitting here, I feel..." She looked around like she was searching for the right word. "Comfortable. For the first time in a really long time. I've missed that. I hadn't realized how much until now." Her voice grew faint. "Living with Trevor in his mansion can be a bit intense." She shifted her weight in the chair. "I'm sure you've noticed that he tends to get his way."

Ben nodded. "That certainly appears to be the pattern." He'd met Trevor at his sire, Christopher's coronation, and after just a few minutes of conversation, Trevor arranged to be Ben's patron so Ben could focus on his inventions and not have to worry about logistics. It was all done, with Ben moved in by the pool, in less than a week. That was a year ago, and the time had flown by. "How did you two meet?"

"We met at a museum; they were hosting some sort of gala." Lauren waved her hand dismissively. "Trevor was handsome, charming, rich, and exactly what I was looking for."

Ben raised his eyebrows in surprise.

"I'm not ashamed I'm a career wife," Lauren said. "Some people are really good at building bridges, or flying planes, or doing heart surgery. I just happen to be very good at taking care of a husband." She shrugged her shoulders. "It's just easier for me to do my job if the husband happens to be rich."

"You'll get no judgement from me. For whatever that's worth," Ben said.

"Thanks." Lauren smiled. "Trevor kind of swept me off my feet, to be honest. He was so put-together and smart; he always had the perfect quip at hand, the exact right thing to say in any scenario. We'd go on a date together, and he'd surprise me by flying us to Paris. Lazy weekends on private yachts, private stays at exclusive resorts, helicopter rides over the city..." She sighed. "It was magic. One thing led to another, and now I'm a vampire." She stood up quickly, putting down the pizza and wandering down the center of the room. "What about you? How'd you become a vampire?"

Ben swallowed a bite of pizza quickly so he could speak without peppering Lauren with cheesy spit. "I grew up in Barbados, mid-nineteenth century. Christopher, my sire, found me fixing a broken sugar distiller. You should have seen my face, I was so sure he was going to call down the overseers and have me whipped again." Ben held up his dark-skinned hands. "People who looked like me weren't supposed to be smart, and my owners tended to shoot first and ask questions later." Lauren's mouth hung slightly open in shock, her pizza forgotten for the moment, and Ben hurried on. "But Christopher did no such thing. He offered to sire me, to keep me safe, so I could improve the world with my mechanical knowledge."

"That's quite a debt. No pressure or anything," Lauren said.

"I've come up with a *few* contraptions here and there." He dusted off a blueprint for a self-driving bicycle and showed it to Lauren. "Now I'm trying to focus my work. I'm hoping to do Christopher proud and solve some of the pesky world problems that keep popping up."

Lauren asked, "I imagine a pool house isn't the ideal setup for your work?"

"The conditions aren't ideal, but it's convenient. I can be a bit scatterbrained at times, and I haven't got a head for business at all." Ben pointed at the pneumatic tube running from the east wing of Trevor's house, along the side of the pool held up by spindly columns, and ending at a small station on the lab table closest to the wall. "Trevor takes care of everything: funding, lab supplies, and getting my inventions out to the world so they can be *used*. All I have to do is send him a note like this." Ben scrawled 'beakers' on a scrap of paper and popped it into a plastic cylinder. He placed it into the tube, and with a 'woosh', it flew away towards the mansion.

Lauren watched the paper disappear into the house and her face paled. She looked at her watch and jumped to her feet.

"Trevor will be wondering where I've gone. I should be heading back. I'll see you the next time I send a confused pizza guy your way."

He was usually in a rush to get people out of his lab. But, for some reason, he didn't want Lauren to leave. She had a kind face, but he couldn't think of any reason for her to stay.

"Until next time," he said.

"Catch you later, secret pizza buddy." And with a wink, she was gone.

LAUREN SMILED to herself as she pulled open the ridiculously ornate door of Trevor's mansion. If she hadn't needed a safe space to eat pizza, it's possible she would have never investigated the pool house at all. And, whatever she'd expected to be out there, Ben wasn't it. She'd taken for granted that all vampires were like Trevor: pale, aloof, and as timeless as a classic movie. But Ben was *present*, his energy so huge his flailing hands could barely contain it. And yet he also had a calming, grounded quality Lauren associated with personal trainers and manicurists.

And--as much as it embarrassed her to admit it to herself-- she hadn't really thought that *of course* there would be black vampires. *And this one has sweet eyes and great hands--*

"Where were you?"

She held her jaw stiff to hide the wince. Trevor's voice grated more than usual after the easiness of being around Ben. Trevor walked down the curving, stone steps, his body framed by the ancient tapestries that lined the wall. The edges of the ancient fabric were frayed, the colors fading from lack of protection from the elements.

"I was walking outside," Lauren said. *Technically* not a lie. She had walked outside from the pool house back to the house. Trevor had never mentioned Ben, just that the pool house was filled with a bunch of his old things. That had been back when she first moved in, getting the grand tour of the Gothic mansion where Trevor insisted she spend all her time. Back then, he'd still been phrasing his words broadly. *The outside world can be dangerous, so don't wander about.* Words which were vague enough to give her the freedom to go almost anywhere. Lauren was becoming a quick study in the many interpretations of commands.

"I'm so happy to see you, my love. You looked stressed. How can I help?" she said quickly, before Trevor asked any more questions.

"Come here." Trevor pointed to the bottom of the stairs.

Lauren's body locked, the *hortari* taking hold as his words controlled her body, forcing her steps closer to him. She resisted, hoping this would be the time her body actually obeyed her, rather than her sire. Her heart hammered in her chest. Lauren's feet moved on their own accord across the room, each movement mechanical, making her feel off balance and a stranger in her own skin.

It was always like this with him, and Lauren choose to lean into the command, taking long, calming breaths before letting her legs swing forward one at a time. She'd never forget the first time the *hortari* locked in on her. She'd only been a vampire for a day, experimenting with her new abilities. The main hall had called to her, the four-story arched ceilings giving her plenty of space to see just how high her newly-strengthened legs could jump.

The feeling had been extraordinary: like flying, each jump sending her higher. A few more leaps and she was sure she'd be able to touch the ceiling. Then Trevor had walked in, told her to stop hopping around like a child and be still. She plunged to the floor, her feet fusing to the ground. No matter how she pulled, they wouldn't move until he gave her permission.

The house was even colder than the night outside; the gray walls with the narrow windows were placed so high they barely let in any moonlight, and kept the cold trapped inside. The enormous fireplaces, built for roaring fires taller than her, lay dark and cold. She knew vampires didn't require warmth, but everything about this place made her shiver, inside and out, and, day by day, it wasn't getting any better.

Her feet carried her across the rest of the room, stopping when they'd arrived at the spot on the floor where Trevor pointed. The moment the order was complete, she relaxed, the *hortari*'s spell broken for the moment. Lauren smiled at her boyfriend and sire.

"Yes, dear?" The endearment sounded a little forced, but she managed to make her smile look genuine. She'd had friends whose husbands had taken a couple of years to manage. She had centuries with Trevor to figure it out. Stick it out long enough, she knew she'd bend him back around her finger.

He spread a handkerchief on top of the wooden banister

along the side of the stairs, the white fabric coming away gray with dust. "This house is filthy. You used to love to clean for me."

When was this? Lauren had always tidied up after herself, but she'd never gone out of her way to clean the dozens of rooms in Trevor's palatial mansion. She'd certainly never claimed to *love* cleaning, that's for sure.

In the last month, Lauren had asked him twice about the house's staff, but she had yet to see another soul. This house was *huge*, there had to be people to clean it, maintain the furnishings, and care for the grounds. During the first couple of weeks, she'd heard the sounds of cleaners during the day while she slept, but in the last few weeks, those sounds had stopped, and dust was beginning to show.

"Perhaps, if you'd like, I could make some calls. I'm quite the expert at finding good help." She stepped forward to lay a hand gently on his arm. He liked it when she touched him without being told to. "If the staff you used weren't what you preferred, I know of a great cleaning service. I'd love to look into at least some part-time staff to spruce up the grounds. Perhaps--"

"Lauren." He patted her hand against his arm, leaning forward to cup her face. "I want *you* to be the one to take care of our home."

Oh fuck. That's way too unspecific. Blood drained from her face, but Lauren latched onto her smile and held onto it like a life raft. She could see it like a premonition: her body locked into cleaning this house for the rest of eternity, unable to sleep or eat in a constant fight against dust in this enormous, fucking house. *Take care of* could be interpreted as *hiring staff*. She let out a deep breath. *I can make this work. He just wants to see he's in control.*

"Of course, my love. Where would you like me to start?"

Trevor smiled. "The bookshelf in my bedroom. You could learn a few things from my prize possessions. Dust them, care for them." He grasped her chin, pointing her face upward like he might kiss her. "They deserve your *respect*." Tiny flecks of spittle hit her face. Her smile didn't waver.

"I understand." The words had barely left her lips and her body was already pulling away, forced inexorably upstairs toward Trevor's bedroom. Behind her, Trevor's laugh was high-pitched and shrill.

"That's my good girl."

The relentless drive of the *hortari* eased slightly when she reached Trevor's bedroom. Lauren didn't have the slightest idea where Trevor kept cleaning supplies, so she grabbed one of his shirts from the bottom of his frightening large laundry pile (they *really* needed to hire some help, this was getting ridiculous), and faced his bookshelf.

She hadn't known a lot about Bram Stoker's *Dracula* before she moved in with Trevor, but she now knew far more than she ever wished. Trevor had somehow tracked down a copy of every single of the one thousand, twenty-nine editions. His custom-built bookshelf for his collection was carved with the words,

Listen to them, the children of the night. What music they make!

She picked up the shirt and ran the fabric over the words, partially to block them from view.

When she first moved in, she'd read the book, since it was so clearly one of Trevor's favorites. "Ugh." The small noise of disgust was soft, too soft for anyone to hear, but still satisfying. Horror just wasn't her thing, but she tried to like Trevor's favorite book for his sake.

Dust them, care for them. The dust command was easy. Her hand moved on its own accord, the fabric running in a cursory fashion along the spines, across the top of the books, and the inch of wood in front while barely touching them. She didn't need to dust *well*, just dust enough for the *hortari's* satisfaction. *Care for them* was too vague to require anything specific from her, and thankfully, *hortari* couldn't force her to *feel* anything even as abstract as *caring*. For someone who threw out *hortari* commands as often as Trevor, Lauren thanked the stars every day he was so imprecise with it.

In so many ways, her life could be so much worse, she reminded herself as her hands dusted one row of books, then the next without her guidance. She and Trevor kept separate bedrooms, for one. The sex at the restaurant before he turned her had been great, but then she'd needed a few days for her body to transition to vampire. She'd been laid up in a guest bedroom as every limb felt like it weighed a hundred pounds, and her vision swam in and out like a bad high. Once she was up to full, supernatural strength, able to leap over trees and hear the clicking of every spider crawling along the ceiling, he'd said he would wait until she was ready to move bedrooms.

She gave the top of the books a good, long swipe. *I know you'll beg me for it eventually,* he had said to her, smirking his no-teeth smile. She'd been ready to jump back into some hot vampire sex until he said those words. There was a malice there she hadn't seen before and it scared her. Then his constant commands started up, and she welcomed any excuse to stay away. For all his *eternal bride of the night* line, they weren't married, and it was as good a reason as any to insist she keep Trevor at arms-length as long as she could.

She sighed. *I'm just delaying the inevitable.* Lauren knew how this worked. She lived in his house, drank the blood he provided. An arrangement like that was never free, and without a budget to prove she could adequately run a large home, there was only one thing she would eventually have to do to keep from getting kicked to the curb.

I can do this. With her eyes closed she could imagine it was anyone there with her in the dark. Perhaps someone a little taller, with kind eyes, dark skin, and enormous hands which touched even a wrench with reverence. Perhaps someone who looked at each moment with such wide-eyed wonder and surprise, and talked about a truly horrific past as if it was just a bad dream. It would be so easy to imagine Ben's mouth against her skin, all that huge energy focused on her, his tongue between her legs, sweeping up her slit and sucking on her bud...

Her hand stopped moving. She'd reached the last row of the bookshelf without even noticing. She relaxed, the muscles of her arm sore from moving for so long with no relief. The dusting was complete, the *hortari* broken. She slumped against the wall, leaning her head down to her knees. Imagining being with Ben was pointless. He was a penniless inventor. He was just as dependent on Trevor as she was, and looked at his test tubes with more affection than he looked at her.

"Darling, you don't have to wait for me on the floor," Trevor said as he entered the room. He was all smiles now, dressed in a tuxedo Lauren remembered from one of their fancier dates. She'd thought he looked like James Bond at the time, but now--she blamed her newly-enhanced vampire senses—but he looked like the shifty butler in a murder mystery.

She shook her head. Trevor was her boyfriend, she wanted to like him. She *needed* to like him.

"I bought you something," Trevor said.

"Oh?" The phrase used to make her so happy, why didn't it any more?

He danced back to his closet and emerged with a cerulean, floor-length dress of clinging silk that draped down so low in the back and front it could have been couture overalls.

"Thank you." Lauren got to her feet. The dress would require some high maintenance throughout the night to stay on her body, but she'd been sure to move in with all her specially-designed underwear and body tape in hope of gifts just like this. She ran a hand down the smooth fabric. It was beautiful.

"We're going to the opera tonight. I want you to wear this."

Lauren smiled at him. The *I want* meant it was still her choice, and even if the opera had never been her favorite, an invitation to get out of the house for the first time since she moved in was a delightful new development. Putting in the effort to making it work would be a good first step to getting them back on track.

It took a couple of hours to get her makeup, hair, and cleavage in place and then they were off. Stepping out of his limo and walking hand-in-hand up the red-carpeted staircase into the opera house was like stepping back onto familiar footing.

This was what she knew how to do. She smiled to a couple of witches she'd been friendly with when she was married to Nikolai, and waved across the room to a trio of tiger shifters who regularly and famously would make love in their opera box while the show was going on.

Her smile broadened. Lauren hadn't gone further than the pool house since she'd been turned, but being out among people as a vampire was fascinating. When she was married to Nikolai, she'd have to wait until after introductions for her bear to explain that so-and-so was a cursed Viking or a pixie or a troll, but here she could smell it all in their blood. And so much more. With one inhalation, she knew who was at the show out of forbearance for a loved one, who was keeping up appearances as cultured, and who was genuinely interested in the show (true of more people than she'd anticipated). The tiger shifters' arousal and anticipation of getting under each other's clothes was so palpable she could smell it at thirty feet, but with the way they were eyeing each other, vampire senses weren't necessary to know what they would do once the curtain rose.

"My past love, Felicity, she adored the opera," Trevor said suddenly. He was glancing around the red and gold room, his gaze skimming the chandeliers as big as a car and the modern art which, laid on its size, would be bigger than the layout of the house Lauren grew up in.

"Oh?"

He turned to her, fixing her with one of his pale, blue-eyed stares. "You remind me so much of her. Felicity was breathtaking, so graceful and poised, a true lady through and through, quiet and calm and comforting. Felicity understood true beauty..."

Lauren's attention wandered. He'd mentioned his ex a couple of times, but never waxed on quite so rhapsodically before. *It must be this place.* She'd come to the opera plenty of times with Nikolai when he needed to entertain out of town guests from other shifter clans. Every corner still held memories: of Nikolai bringing her a glass of her favorite wine, of charming his guests when Nikolai accidentally offended someone. The ghost of Nikolai's hand resting as a comfortable weight on the small of her back followed her through the lobby. Trevor's hands were busy with his drink, his fingers caressing his glass as he reminisced, his voice pointed to the walls.

"Felicity was so beautiful in red, you should have seen her--"

"Darling, they're calling us to take our seats," Lauren interrupted. The chimes rang out once more, warning the show was about to start, and Lauren slipped her arm through Trevor's, steering him toward the theater's doors.

"Ah yes, I hadn't realized. Thank you. You really are quite conscientious, Lauren. So like Felicity."

How complementary. She bit back the words from leaving her mouth just in time. Trevor hated sarcasm.

They reached their seats: a private box to the side of the stage with a great view of the entire set as well as the (far more interesting) view into the wings where the sets and actors waited to go on.

Make this work, she reminded herself. She glanced at Trevor and relaxed a little. He was smiling, leaning back in his chair with one arm draped behind her chair in an intimate gesture.

"Trevor, darling. When I used to come to the opera with friends, there was a game we used to play to help pass the time." Even if he didn't know about Nikolai--*being a widow automatically makes a woman sound old*--there wasn't any reason why they couldn't play. She raised her wine glass to him. "You take a drink whenever there's a trap door, or someone holds a note longer than ten seconds, or--"

"That is unsophisticated." Trevor cut her off. He withdrew his arm from the back of her chair. "You may not play that game."

The *hortari* settled in her hands like an itch against her skin. "But--"

"And you will not talk about it."

Her throat closed up, her words freezing in her throat.

Not good, not good at all.

The curtain lifted, and the attention of the audience shifted toward the stage, but the figures and music were a blur in front of Lauren's eyes. Tears formed and she blinked them back. She missed Nikolai. She missed the solid strength of him, the dry humor he saved just for her during the quiet moments between clan meetings and networking events when it was just the two of them. The opera game hadn't just

been because neither of them knew Italian and the histri-
onics on the stage were repetitive and lasted too long, it was
about having something private that they could share
together, even in the midst of a crowd.

Ben would understand. She wasn't sure where the thought
came from, but she pushed it away.

A trap door on the stage lifted up, raising a woman wearing a
headdress that looked like a cross between a sailboat and bull
horns, all painted gold.

Trap door, take a drink, she toasted in her head, then raised her
glass to take a sip.

Her hand wouldn't move.

Trevor was glaring at the stage, his arms crossed tight across
his chest.

The *hortari* banning her from playing a harmless drinking
game wouldn't allow her to raise her glass to her lips. She
waited a moment, then took a long gulp of her wine. *Of
course, once it's not about the game, then I can drink.*

Lauren sat seething for the rest of the act. She had secreted
some blood bags in her clutch, and poured some into her
glass once her wine was done. She concentrated on the taste
of it sliding down her throat, trying to find some sense of
calm. She'd chosen this bag because it was from a giddy
dragon shifter who donated it during her honeymoon, and
Lauren had hoped the excitement of new love in the blood
would help make the evening more enjoyable. But the
contrast between her own feeling--wanting to club Trevor
over the head--was so extremely different from the dragon's

happiness. The taste just made her slump deeper into her chair.

The curtain dropped and the lights turned on signaling intermission. For the first time in her life, Lauren wished the first act had continued a little longer.

Trevor's grip clenched around her hand, hard enough the fine bones of her fingers ground together.

"Darling, you're hurting--" she started to say.

"We're leaving." He pulled her to her feet with a sharp tug, dragging her so fast she missed her footing and fell onto the booth's carpeting. As she fell, she smacked her elbow hard on wooden rail, a shock of pain spiking through her body. Trevor didn't wait for her to get up, sighing exasperatedly as he stalked away, calling over his shoulder for her to "come along, quickly."

The *hortari* kicked in, and there wasn't time to be graceful. Lauren kicked off her shoes, threw aside the front of her skirt to get to her feet as fast as possible. Without her commanding them to, her bare feet dashed after Trevor's rapidly retreating form. Lauren gave one last glance back at their opera box. In the struggle, one of the chairs had knocked over, shattering one of the glasses of blood. Her abandoned shoes were splattered with the red, ruined. She caught up with Trevor halfway down the hallway.

"Felicity would have enjoyed tonight," he muttered, so low she wouldn't have heard it without the enhanced hearing of a vampire. "I've seen this bloody show a million times. I did this for *you*."

They made it through the winding corridors of the old hall, down the stairs, and through the exit of the building before most of the other audience members had gotten out of their seats.

"Are we leaving?" Lauren asked as they passed the front doors. The marble steps out front froze her toes, but she was too scared to complain. "Trevor, talk to me."

"What is there to talk about? You're without any grace, any class. You have no appreciation for the finer things, Felicity, the things that *I* provide for you. Do you know how much I've sacrificed for you? Don't you realize that what I've given you, *all* I've given you, is a gift to show my undying adoration?"

"Trevor, you're scaring me. *I'm* Lauren." She had to run to keep up with him. She touched his arm gently. "Trevor, I'm Lauren."

He glanced at her, then away. He didn't slow until they reached the parking lot and waved down their driver. Trevor pushed her into the back seat. Fear pulsed at her, quick and hot.

"Shut up, and stay still," Trevor said.

Inside her head, she screamed. Lauren wanted to yell at Trevor for being such an ass, cut him with her words for mortifying her in front of the society she had struggled so hard to join. How many saw her fall in that booth? How many witnessed her fleeing barefoot out to the car? How could she show her face in front of any of them again?

But she couldn't move. Couldn't speak. Only her heart beat

fast in her chest, pushing out blood to fuel her body for a screaming match she couldn't speak.

She glanced out the window, at the running lights on the ceiling of the car, anywhere but at the man next to her saying that she looked lovely tonight, and wasn't it nice when they weren't fighting?

I can't do this.

"So... how was your date last night?" Ben asked. He'd seen Trevor and Lauren dressed to the nines as they headed out the night before. He'd never seen anyone look so lovely in blue, even if he thought Lauren looked even more enchanting in her sweater and jeans.

Lauren shook her head. "I don't want to talk about it."

She'd ducked into his pool house lab the second the sun set that night, only relaxing once she'd shut the door behind her. It had taken Ben a few minutes to figure out how to order pizza using his phone, but a half-hour later she was laughing with bits of bacon stuck to the front of her sweater.

Ben let out a slow breath, trying to keep his hands from shaking as he delicately lowered the final membrane into his device.

"Stay down," he warned as the thin membrane fluttered in the almost non-existent breeze.

"Trust me, I am going nowhere near *that*," Lauren said through a mouthful of spinach and artichoke pizza. She had ducked beneath one of Ben's many lab tables, and had begun to create a small fort out of sheets of metal and boxes of supplies, more to mock Ben's 'mad science' than for actual protection. She peered out of her hiding spot. "Be honest, how many interdimensional portals have you created by accident? Just like, a ballpark."

A chuckle escaped Ben's lips. "Don't make me laugh." He hissed, afraid to speak at a normal volume. Having Lauren in the lab with him made everything more exciting, more *real*. He'd certainly never been in danger of messing up an experiment before due to a case of the giggles. It was odd, but Ben liked it.

Ben gently moved the membrane, made out of a new polymer he invented for the occasion. It had a tendency to burst into flame if introduced to water too quickly, but--if he settled it right--could help increase the rotator's efficiency. He steadied his forceps and inched it downward.

"Ben!" Trevor's voice called out from outside. The pool door swung open hard, banging against the wall.

Ben jumped, losing his grip and dropping the membrane into his latest desalinator. A plume of flame shot into the air, the fire barely missing Ben's face, and he dove for cover.

Lauren's yelp of alarm was hidden by the siren from the sprinkler system creaking to life, erupting water from the overhead taps. Rain soaked the pool house, extinguishing the fire. Ben glanced around noting Lauren was safe under the table, his computer was covered in protective plastic, and anything else of any real value was down in his bedroom in the basement.

"Visiting you is always interesting, old boy." Trevor's long, black cape over a black and silver velvet suit was drenched, along with the stack of paper in his hand. Ben realized he was sopping wet as well, water dripping down his face as Trevor dumped the waterlogged pages into a nearby trash can.

"I *was* bringing you some routine paperwork from the investors, but it appears I will need to recreate these forms for you."

Trevor seemed to be a good mood, Ben was curious to see. Lauren was still hiding out of sight rather than coming out to greet her boyfriend, and Ben wasn't sure what that could imply about his nephew. As Danny's sireling, Trevor was one generation removed from Christopher, but their whole sire line was known for their empathy, creativity, and good-will toward others. It was what made them different from Ben's uncle, Rhys and all of his *hortari*-abusing sirelings. If Trevor wasn't being kind to his sirelings, Ben would certainly have to inform the king. But he needed more evidence than an uneasiness in his gut before he acted. *And yet...*

"Sorry about that." Ben waved vaguely at his charred experiment. "Volatile polymer, you know how it is."

"Actually I don't." Trevor dusted off a wooden stool, sweeping aside his cloak with all the drama of a middle school thespian. Ben smiled. *This* was his awkward, overly-dramatic nephew. Any uneasiness Ben felt was probably just because Trevor was a bit of an odd duck.

Trevor steepled his fingers beneath his chin. "Tell me. How's your latest project going?"

"I'm still perfecting my desalinator." Ben pulled a rolled up blueprint off of a stack of wires and rubber tubing. Out of the corner of his eye, Lauren shrunk further into her hiding spot. *Their relationship isn't my business,* he told himself, pushing aside his unease.

Trevor swiped the blueprints out of Ben's hand, running his fingers down the page and making little comments of 'uh huhs' and 'mmm...interesting'.

"Trevor..." Ben waved around the enormous sheet of paper that was blocking Trevor's view. "That's upside down."

Trevor glared at him, his expression switching from friendly to furious in less than a second.

Whoa. Ben stepped back.

"How dare you hand me upside down blueprints. I give you everything you need to work on your fancies, and you try to make a fool out of me?" Trevor's voice growled.

"But...you took the blueprints *from--*" Ben sputtered.

"Never mind that. Let me see how far you've gotten with my money."

"Right. Um." Ben pulled out his beloved machine, giving the already shining gears a little extra rub for luck. "This one's the most promising model so far. I just put some plastic waste, like this water bottle, into this input here." He pulled open a compartment about the size of a banana and stuffed in a crumpled up bottle. "And add in some ocean water here." He poured from a jug of collected ocean water into a funnel. "And voila!" Ben pressed a big, red button, and the device began to shake, letting out a terrible, grinding sound. The instruments on the lab table all bounced along with the box's vibrations.

"Just another few seconds of this!" Ben shouted above the din.

"Stop that terrible noise!" Trevor screamed, covering his ears.

A happy "ding!" rang out and the machine stopped. Ben pulled two glass vials from the side of the box.

"Here's our good news and our bad news," Ben said. "We end up with potable drinking water, but also this second vial of waste."

Trevor grabbed the brown byproduct and took a long sniff at the top, then smiled. "Gasoline is *not* waste." Trevor slapped Ben on the shoulder. "You've done it! You've found a way to convert plastics into gasoline!'"

Ben frowned. "I found a way to use plastics to convert ocean water into water safe to drink."

"Right, right. This is amazing." Trevor hadn't stopped looking at the gasoline, his longing making Ben increasingly uncomfortable.

Ben gently removed the vial from Trevor's hand. "I'm still working on the prototype. With each version, I'm making it more efficient, maximizing the amount of drinking water that's output while minimizing the gasoline runoff."

Trevor jumped to his feet. "Don't do that. This machine is great just as it is. I predict we'll be able to make this available to investors in just a few weeks. With my business expertise and your science, we will be *unstoppable*. You, me, and my lady are going to go all the way with this one, just you watch."

My lady. Ben knew he was frowning and tried to smooth his expression. The way Trevor said the words sent a chill down Ben's spine.

"So, how are things between you and your newest lady?" Aware that Lauren was within earshot, Ben chose his words carefully.

Trevor grinned. "I think I finally found the one in Lauren."

"That's wonderful. But it's not the first time I've heard you say that about a girlfriend." *At least the last three*, Ben didn't say.

"Those cows I courted before Lauren didn't know how to really take care of a man. Lauren has enormous potential. I'm certain I'll be able to mold her into what I need." Trevor sneered.

A sneer isn't evidence that something is wrong, Ben reminded himself. He was a scientist. He needed *proof*. "Your last girlfriend, Susan, I think, was nice. She'd sing by the pool sometimes. Whatever happened with her?" Ben cautiously probed.

Trevor shifted his weight, looking at the ground. "You could say I gave her some flowers and sent her on her way." He nodded, making steely eye contact with Ben. "Yes. That's exactly what I did."

Trevor's words were innocent enough, but his tone made the hairs on the back of Ben's neck stick up. Each second of silence that passed was exponentially more awkward than the one before it.

"Speaking of business." Ben nodded at his wet, ash-covered workbench.

"Right. I'll leave you to it, then." Trevor moved towards the door. "I'll be back with a drier version of that paperwork for you to sign. Standard stuff." With a sweep of his cape, he was gone.

"Thanks for not ratting me out." Lauren's voice was small and low from under the table.

"No problem, but..." Ben fiddled with some clear pipettes, twirling them between his fingers. "Why were you hiding from Trevor? He's your sire *and* your boyfriend. Aren't you two getting along?" Ben asked.

"I think I made a mistake." Lauren fixed her hair, looking everywhere but at Ben. "I thought I knew what I was getting myself into when I let Trevor turn me." She straightened up. "Being with him is...complicated." She laughed nervously. "Ugh. If I was human, I would so need a drink right now."

Ben beamed, excited to have the solution so easily at hand. "I know just the place. AUDREY'S. You'll love it." He moved towards the door, his wet shoes squishing against the floor.

"I would absolutely love to, but I can't." Lauren slumped. "I'm not allowed to. Trevor's used the *hortari* to prevent me from leaving the grounds unsupervised." She shrugged. "I'm stuck here."

"Hardly." Ben guided her to the door. "I'll keep an eye on you. Surely the *hortari* would consider me a responsible adult?"

"Oh, absolutely," Lauren said solemnly. Her eyes twinkled, and the hint of a smile grew on her lips.

"Good. Then come with me, I'll keep you safe." Ben desperately hoped it was true.

LAUREN HADN'T BEEN in a dive bar since high school when she used to sneak into the college bars with a fake ID. The off-balance stools and stained tables she passed reassured Lauren this was a place where she could relax, and vying for status here wouldn't matter. She'd been to a few places that catered to the supernatural set--Nikolai's favorite cocktail lounge was in a glitzy ice hotel owned by a bear shifter and a witch--but she'd never been anywhere quite so *enthusiastic* about embracing what most humans considered impossible.

"What is this place?" she asked Ben as they made their way to a cozy booth in the back. Her hand clamped tightly around his arm, even if the cramped space made it difficult to walk arm in arm.

"This is AUDREY'S. It's a bar for people like us. It was opened by the witch grandmother of the current owner, Audrey." He nodded toward a red-haired witch standing next to the bartender, scanning through an enormous, ancient-looking tome behind the bar.

"It's, um--"

Ben smiled, handing her a flyer of that week's events. "Careful. Rumor is, this place is a little bit alive, so you wouldn't want to insult it."

"I wasn't!" What she'd intended to say was *interesting*, which probably wasn't the best move if the bar was sensitive. "It's *lovely*. Everyone seems to be having a lot of fun."

A horse shifter brayed with joy as she wheeled out an old karaoke machine and quickly set it up in the center of the bar.

Looking around, Lauren had never seen so many supernaturals in one place. The place was packed with pixies, yetis, dragon shifters, werewolves, bear shifters, and witches, all together in mixed groups around the rickety tables. There was even a woman whose body was entirely made of intertwining swamp grasses and sticks wearing a lab coat, glasses, and nothing else.

Cheers rang out (with a few interspersed, good-natured groans) as the karaoke machine sprang to life and folks handed forward pieces of paper to sign-up to sing.

Lauren gave Ben a speculative glance and he laughed, holding up his hands. "Trust me, you don't want to hear me sing. I'm an off-key fog horn."

A very pale hand slid forward to deposit two drinks on their table. "Oh sweetie, you think there is actually going to be singing? Just you watch." Lola the bartender--a pale woman with disarmingly red lips, a rose tattoo across her entire chest, and hundreds of small braids surrounding her head--grinned into Lauren's eyes. Lauren's shoulders relaxed a little just being near her. The woman wasn't a vampire, but Lauren couldn't identify what Lola was even when Lauren leaned unnecessarily close to shake the woman's hand. Something old and odd, but that was all she could smell.

Lola nodded to the glass in front of Lauren. "That's my patented calm down juice. Just don't ask what's in it."

Lauren glanced down at her drink. It definitely had blood in it, she could smell a sense of the donor's calm and wellbeing, but the drink was bright purple and steamed a little.

Ben looked at his glass. "Am I allowed to ask?" He held it up to the light, and gave an experimental sniff.

Lola laughed. "Don't worry, you have your usual. Blood donated by a science fair winner, your favorite. With just a splash of tequila."

"Thanks!" He replied with such enthusiasm, Lauren giggled.

"Everyone! Tonight I will be your Master of Karaoke!" The bar's owner, Audrey, stood at the microphone, her arms raised above her head. The room cheered. She held up a clear bowl filled with the dozen or so cards which had already been filled out. "You all know the rules, but a quick reminder: pass up your cards if you want a turn and *don't* be the asshole who volunteers your friends without their okay." She smiled broadly to the room and dug her hand deep into the bowl, withdrawing a card. "And our first up is Shelby Meyer, singing 'Niveis Incantamentum'!"

The whole room cheered and made good natured cat calls as a tiger shifter wearing tight, black leather came to the front of the room.

Lauren leaned forward to whisper to Ben, "I've never heard of that song. What language is that?"

Ben smiled and tapped his nose. "You'll see."

The tiger shifter pressed play on the tablet at the front of the small stage and words that looked like a mix of Latin and esoteric symbols projected onto the wall behind her. Music swelled through the speakers, a fast drum beat with soaring violins playing a tune that Lauren didn't recognize, but knew she'd be humming for the next week. A bouncing ball on the screen beat out a countdown to when the words started. Lauren felt herself being drawn forward toward the words. The air tasted thicker, with strange currents moving along her skin that tickled and cooled all at once. She glanced at Ben, who was already grinning with delight.

The woman started to sing, her voice not entirely on key, but following the words with perfect ease and a confidence that made it easy not to notice that her tune didn't quite line up with the violins. Lauren couldn't understand the words, but as the tiger shifter sang, the room dropped in temperature and all around the bar, couples cuddled closer together and grinned, looking up and around in anticipation of something.

Lauren eyed Ben. He was so big, looked so warm. Would he welcome it if she just slid a little closer to soak in some of his heat? Every time she'd gone by the pool house, he'd always worn that oversized lab coat which completely hid his body. But before they left to come to the bar, he'd changed into a clean t-shirt right there in front of her: whipping off his lab coat, removing the grease-stained shirt he'd been wearing underneath, and revealing an incredible set of washboard abs, surprisingly ripped arms, and a beautifully-muscled back which narrowed down at his waist in a delectable trian-gle. She'd barely been able to breathe, and now that she knew the glory hidden beneath his lab coats, the temptation to snuggle up a little beckoned like an itch.

The music swelled and the tiger shifter swayed her hips, her fingers twirling like she was playing a piano in the air to the song's beat.

Something small and white hit Lauren's nose and she looked up.

Snow! Snow was falling from the ceiling in perfect, crystalline flakes. It swirled around the room in spiraling eddies that danced to the tune of the music.

"This is amazing!" Lauren cried, her voice lost in the cheers and applause from around the room.

Ben grinned and slid his chair over next to her with a look of pure bliss on his face. It took just the smallest movement and Lauren's head rested on his shoulder, her side lightly brushing his side.

"*This* is how magic is supposed to be," he said.

Lauren nodded, his shoulder brushing the side of her face as her head moved. *This is how love is supposed to be.* The thought came, sudden and unwelcome. She pushed it down, sitting up straight. Ben wasn't an option. He was her friend, and she was with Trevor.

The song slowed, the tempo calming, and the tiger lowered her arms, her singing growing soft. The room warmed, the snowflakes vanished one by one like tiny stars winking out, and the music lulled to silence. As the song ended, Lauren clapped enthusiastically, joined by everyone else in the room. She didn't look at Ben, hoping her face wasn't blushing as furiously as she thought it was.

I cannot be falling in love with Ben.

The tiger shifter made her way back to her table, getting high-fives, thumbs up, and slaps on the back all the way to her chair, and Audrey jumped back onto the stage. The red-haired witch pulled another card from the bowl and the swamp-grass woman swayed up to the mic when her name was called. Lauren took a sip of her purple drink, feeling calm and a deep joy settle in her bones. The comfort reminded her of pizza, of her folding chair at the pool house, and Ben's eyes.

"This is a lullaby of my people." The woman's voice was rasping and low like the sound of the wind through tall grasses. When she pressed play on the tablet, calming plinks of harps and a plonking ring of what Lauren guessed was some kind of xylophone emerged from the speakers. As the woman sang, ghostlike images emerged to hang in the air above their heads. Grassy hills and trees against brilliant sunsets floated and bumped together like they were suspended in enormous bubbles.

"Thank you for bringing me here," Lauren said in a low voice to Ben. "I thought I knew everything there was to know about the supernatural world after all those years being the wife of a bear shifter, but there's *so* much."

Ben nodded. "More than can be seen or experienced in a hundred lifetimes. My brother, Danny, was an explorer for a few centuries, and tried to see everything in the world. He found that by the time he'd gotten all the way around the world, where he'd been had already changed. There's always new things to see. Now he's running a club with his fiancé, but does investigations for our sire, the king, that take him all over the world."

She wanted to ask about what an investigator did. Traveling around the world discovering new things sounded great. But she latched onto the most important piece of information. "Your sire is the *king*? You're a *prince*?"

Ben shrugged. A floating image of a mountainside crowned with clouds bounced against his head like a balloon before joining its fellows dancing around the rafters. "Christopher turned me long before he was king. He's always had a sense of responsibility towards all living things, and makes a point of only turning folks who he thinks will help the world in some way. It's a lot to live up to, but it really fuels me." He sipped thoughtfully at his drink. "I've invented my fair share of gizmos, but the machine I'm working on will do some *real* good. Once we can safely purify water from the oceans as drinkable water, then all drought could be eliminated. Diseases that spread from unclean water will disappear." He was so excited, he practically vibrated in his seat.

"You put me to shame," Lauren said, smiling at him. "You became a vampire to really make a difference. I just did it because..." Her voice trailed off.

"Because why?" His smile was kind, his arm going around her shoulder to pull her close. She relaxed against his arm, feeling the smooth edges of his muscles through her sweater. Lauren wanted to curl even closer, but she held back, keeping what she hoped would only be construed as a companionable cuddle, if such a thing existed.

"Well, I didn't exactly grow up being encouraged to make the world a better place. It's not an excuse, but it's true. As soon as I was walking, my parents squeezed me into puffy dresses and took me on the pageant circuit. I was no better than the prized pig at a state fair."

Lauren's lip curled at a particularly hateful memory of having her scalp burned by curling irons. The pain lingered for days, but no matter how much she cried, her mother just told her to suck it up, since none of the injuries were visible beneath her hair.

"Judges would assess how cute I was, how brightly I could hold a smile, and if my costume walked the right line between jailbait and pedophilia." She could hear the bitterness in her own voice and took a deep breath. The soothing voice of the swamp lady at the mic calmed her until even her toes relaxed. "When I was seven or eight, I got cast in a few commercials for cereal and toothpaste and such, but I never saw any of that money. My parents told friends and family that everything I was earning was going into a college fund, but the cash never made it out of the liquor store. Every time the debts racked up, I got trotted out to earn money. Our survival relied on how pretty I was."

Ben's eyes were bright as he studied her face. He gave her hand a comforting squeeze. "You have so much more than that to offer."

Lauren shrugged. "I wish I'd heard that years ago. When I was nineteen, my parents died in a skiing accident, and I didn't know how to take care of myself. So I guess I just fell back into what I was trained to do." She smiled wanly.

Audrey was back at the podium announcing the next singer, and Lauren startled in her chair. She'd been so focused on her memories, she hadn't even noticed that the swamp lady's song had finished, the image bubbles vanished like they never existed. Next up to the stage was an enormous troll whose head brushed the ceiling. He led the room in a rousing drinking song that seemed to be mostly grunts and "yahoo!" sung at regular intervals. No magical images or spells took shape in the air, but once the whole room got into the song, the entire bar shook and swayed along with the stomping feet.

Ben touched her shoulder. "Want to go outside? Escape this rowdy crew for a bit?"

Lauren nodded. The music had knocked her from the worst of her memories, but she didn't feel up to singing along just yet.

The night was quiet. A long field stretched out back to a line of trees. Scorch marks in the grass and random holes in the ground signaled that AUDREY's backyard was used for a different purpose during the day, but it was abandoned now. The moon was as bright as day to her vampiric vision, and Lauren breathed deep in the safety of the open space.

Ben held out a hand and she took it, walking in companionable silence to the middle of the field and lying beside him flat on her back, looking up at the stars. She felt like a teenager again, sneaking out of her bedroom to meet up with a boy, the stillness of the night full of possibility. Ben's presence was solid next to her, his usually bursting energy contained.

"I know it's not my place to say..." He started to say.

"What?"

"Well, your parents were a bit awful."

Lauren laughed, a highly unladylike snort her mother would have hated. "A bit." She let out a long breath. "They taught me what they believed. My mother would go out of her way to tell me how she pitied women who 'let themselves down' by not wearing makeup to the grocery store. Father taught me to spot a degenerate by jeans worn too low or if a guy sported a tattoo." That hadn't stopped Lauren from dating as many 'degenerate' low-jeans-wearing-tattooed boys in high school as she could find, but that was a story for another day. "It was constantly stated as fact that if I wasn't skinny and pretty and happy and popular, I'd be starving and degraded by the end of the day."

Even now, knowing that she would never age, her fingers itched to check her skin in the mirror for new wrinkles. She'd effectively done what her mother had tried to achieve through all those facelifts and Botox sessions: Lauren had managed to maintain her body forever in a perfect state of almost-youth. The knowledge made her less pleased than she thought it would.

Ben shook his head. "I know a thing or two about being judged based on appearances. I've been black in America for the last few hundred years, after all, but at least I've always been surrounded by people who appreciated what else I could offer."

Lauren gave him a pained smile. "I know my story doesn't really compare. I never suffered any *real* hardship. Nikolai, my first husband, was really sweet. He was a friend of my parents' who I had met a few times when I was younger. His son was already grown and out of the house when my parents died and Nikolai offered me the protection of his income and a home in exchange for being his wife. I said yes. And he was true to his word: he took care of everything. He bought our house, I used his credit cards. We grew to be comfortable with each other, and those were some of my happiest years. But after he died, I felt just...lost. Those three years before I met Trevor were the first time I'd ever really lived on my own. It terrified me to be under my own control."

"Well, tonight's the night. Nobody's telling you what to do right now. What do you wanna do?" Ben asked.

The back door of the bar swung open and music from inside streamed out into the night. The wafting strains of a slow, swinging beat stole out in the darkness, a man's voice smooth and smoky intertwining with the notes.

Lauren stood up and held out her hand to help Ben to his feet. He stood up next to her in one, flowing motion.

"Dance with me." Her parents only let her dance tap routines for her pageant recitals. Nikolai had a bad hip and would just hold her hand as he bobbed his head to the music. She was never free to dance the way she wanted to.

"I'd love to," Ben said. His hands brushed her hand and her hip, his touch light, letting her lead.

The music grew louder, and twinkling lights that changed color as they floated along streamed out of the bar's back door. The lights turned into a flood of rainbow pinpricks of light that shimmered and surged until they blanketed the sky. The music was now coming *from* the lights, surrounding the two of them and lighting up Ben's face in planes of blue and gold that complemented the pink of his lips and the brightness of his eyes.

Lauren smiled up at the lights, then closed her eyes, feeling the music flow through her from her head down to her toes. The beat pulsed deep in her chest, pumping down to her legs and arms, the surge of the music modulating and caressing her as she moved. Her arms floated up above her head, her hips swayed, her feet lifted and twirled in steps she had never learned, but that felt *right*. Her hair tossed, wild and free, with the beat, one hand pressing against Ben's, while she twirled away from him and then back until she could feel his heat, and then twirling away. She kicked out, felt the movement of the air as Ben danced away, moving behind her, but staying close, his hands touching for the comfort of contact, but not guiding.

For once, she didn't care what she looked like, if her movements were graceful or awkward, if Ben was following or staring. It didn't matter. It was her dance, just her and the music, and every note was sweet.

The song continued on, each verse increasing in intensity until the drums hammered into her bones and her feet flew so fast she kicked off the ground and felt it fall away beneath her. She jumped higher and higher, pushing her vampire strength until her head met the twinkling light and, for a moment, they surrounded her face like old friends.

Ben clapped and whooped, and she stopped jumping to take a look at him. His arms were flung in the air alongside her, kicking and jumping with wild abandon, no technique, just joy. She laughed, copying his movements and feeling warmth down to her toes when he twirled, an echo of how she'd been dancing a moment before. They didn't touch, but she sensed his movements like electricity binding their bodies together, the music connecting their hands, their feet, their hips together as one laughing, flapping creature under the twinkling lights above their heads.

The music slowed, the lights dimmed, until they were once again alone under the stars. She moved closer to Ben. His steps mirrored hers until they stood so close, their chests brushed with each breath.

Nobody's telling you what to do right now. What do you wanna do?

Ben's words echoed in her head like a dare. She stared into his face, which locked on hers with an expression of such bare longing and hunger, her breath hitched. She licked her lips to moisten them, her hands moving up to stroke his shoulders and squeeze the muscles gently. The currents between them felt like living things drawing them closer, and she leaned into it, longing for his embrace, wanting to press her lips to the eyelids of his calm eyes, run her fingers along the sides of his smiling lips, feel his hands on her, covering her skin, entering her everywhere.

The crash of a bottle breaking from inside the bar made her jump.

She stepped back, stumbling a little over the grass. *I'm with Trevor. This is wrong.*

Ben leaned forward to steady her, but she put up her hands to brush away his help.

"We can't," she said.

Ben nodded. "I'll drive us back."

THEY DIDN'T SPEAK on the way home, just a quick, "bye," before Lauren slipped into the house. What was there to say? *Thank you for possibly the best night of my life.* It sounded trite, false, like the sort of thing she used to say to Trevor. *I think I'm falling in love with you.* It was too much, too true, and she couldn't say it. Under all those words was a thought she wasn't entirely sure how to voice. She leaned her head against the glass door of the porch and listened to the click of Ben's lab door on the opposite side of the pool.

I'm afraid what Trevor will do to us if he knows.

I SHOULD HAVE KISSED HER. *I shouldn't want to kiss her at all.* Ben's thoughts dueled with each other as he entered his lab. He seethed at her late parents, even her late husband, everyone who had ever had a hand in convincing her that her looks dictated her worth. Ben wanted to protect her, to hold her, to keep her safe not just from everything out in the world, but from the poison installed in her mind. *She's spectacular.*

Ben was halfway through the lab when he stopped short and frowned. Books that were once arranged in a neat stack were scattered on the ground. His blueprints, usually rolled into a pyramid-shaped pile in the corner, were flung all over the place. His pipettes had been moved, and even his lab notebook was missing.

Someone's been sciencing in my lab.

The familiar sound of a glass test tube being crushed under a boot made Ben spin towards the source. Trevor had made it as far as the door, one hand on the handle and the other cradling a stack of blueprints. Ben could see the outline of his lab journal sticking out the back of Trevor's pants. *Is nothing sacred?*

Ben cleared his throat. "Is there something I can help you with?"

Trevor spun, his grip tightening on the blueprints. "I was just going to make digital backups of your work. That fire the other day made me realize you have everything on *paper* in here. Of course, I was going to discuss it with you, I just..." Trevor stammered. "You weren't here. So I figured, since I pay for everything anyway, I'd..." He shrugged.

Ben wanted to believe him. If it wasn't for Trevor's nervously bobbing Adam's apple, or the bead of sweat that was currently making its way down Trevor's temple, he might have.

"That's not the kind of thing you need to sneak around to do." Ben's voice was a low growl.

Trevor paused, nodded. "Quite right. Quite right." Ben wanted to laugh. Trevor assembling thought was like a train struggling to make it up too steep a hill. Ben could almost see the steam coming out of the man's ears from the effort. "Anyway... since I have you here..."

Trevor desperately looked around until his eye fell on the stack of paper he'd brought with him the day before. He picked them out of the trash, smoothing out the top pages, which had since dried and were mostly readable.

"I still need you to sign these. It's nothing important, but if you could..." He flipped to the back page and pointed to a blank signature line. "That would be great."

Ben slid the stack of papers closer, pulling it out of Trevor's grip so he could read the pages hidden by Trevor's hand. As Ben scanned the words, his eyes widened, and his jaw went slack.

"What is this, Trevor? This says that I relinquish *all ownership* of my desalination device. It puts you in complete control of how this machine is used, all the profits from any potential sales, and lists you as the *official owner of this patent.*" Ben clenched his fist, balling up the incriminating document. "*What is this?*" He shouted.

Trevor let out an aggravated sigh. "*This* is business. I'm the one who can figure out how to make money from your gadgets. Do you realize how much certain nations and nation-sized corporations would pay for this machine to never see the light of day?" Trevor paced a short distance, back and forth, a manic smile growing on his face. "*Trillions.* The answer is trillions of dollars." He flipped back to the signature page. "Sign this and we'll be wealthy beyond our wildest dreams."

"No." Ben's voice was quiet, but firm. "We talked about this. You were going to help me *distribute* my gadgets. My machine will provide clean water to those who need it." He ripped the heavy stack of papers in half in a single tear, dropping them into a metal bucket at his feet. "I will *not* allow you to whore out my invention to a bunch of oil companies." Ben grabbed his jar of polymer scraps and threw them into the bucket. "This will be open-source. Available online to anybody who needs it."

Trevor shook his head and sneered, not paying attention. Ben grabbed the jug of ocean water and poured it into the bucket, the polymer igniting in a whoosh of flames that had Trevor scrambling for the door.

"You're insane, you know that?" Trevor ran outside, Ben close on his heels. Ben was older, faster, and snatched the blueprints from under Trevor's arm. The sprinkler system switched on inside the pool house, but Ben ignored it. He held out his hand.

"My lab journal, if you please." Ben gestured meaningfully at the rectangular bulge in the back of Trevor's pants.

"Fine." Trevor pulled the lab journal out of the back of his pants and handed it to Ben. "*I'm* already fabulously wealthy. I'm not the one living off of charity, leeching off of family like some pathetic idealist."

"You're a worm, Trevor. I'll never know why Danny sired you. You're selfish and devious, and you treat Lauren like garbage."

"Hey!" Trevor cut Ben off, the single word slicing through the air. "I only put up with you and your absent-minded professor act since you're my uncle and I don't need Danny on my case. But Lauren is *my* girlfriend." He took a step closer to Ben. "I'm not a fool, you know. She goes on her little walks and comes home reeking of pizza and seawater. You don't trust me around your little toys? Well, I don't trust you around my woman. Stay away from Lauren, and I'll stay away from your gadgets. Deal?" The door slammed behind Trevor as he stomped back up to the main house.

Ben's gaze followed him, his eyes seeking out some sign of Lauren in the house until he realized what he was doing. Trevor was a little shit, but he had a point. Lauren was with Trevor. And she'd made her choice.

He sighed. "Deal."

LAUREN COULD STILL HEAR the music from the twinkling lights in her head as she pushed the outfit she'd worn to AUDREY'S as far down into her laundry hamper as possible and changed into a flowing, lace nightgown that looked like something out of a Gothic novel. Picking up a rag, she pranced over on light feet to Trevor's book case. Dusting was easy enough, didn't require any attention, and was as good an activity as any to appease Trevor's demands.

She hummed bars of music softly to herself, letting her feet dance a little to the beat, her hips swaying as she reached up to move the rag along the top shelves. If she closed her eyes, she could almost picture herself back there now: the coolness of the night sky playing against her skin, and Ben's beloved presence supportive at her side.

A chill ran through her and she knew she was being watched. She stopped moving, the hum dying in her throat. She knew who was standing at the door before she finished turning, his lurking stare so oppressive she could feel it across the room.

"I just had an *interesting* conversation with Ben." Trevor leaned against his bedroom's door frame, his arms crossed. A shiver of fear ran down her spine. His face was so closed, so cold. The way he stood in the shadow, his eyes looked like black holes.

"Oh?" she tried to sound disinterested as her heart hammered in her chest. She was impressed her hand didn't shake, but continued to slide across the book spines.

"He seemed to think that I wasn't treating you well." His voice was a low growl.

"I can't imagine why he'd think something so ridiculous," she said, her voice smooth. "You have a very comfortable home. I have everything I could possibly need, and most importantly, I have *you*. I'm hardly mistreated." She grabbed at one of the sturdier hardback copies of *Dracula* and spun around to face him. "I hadn't even read *Dracula* before I came here. Imagine that. It's such a *great* book, and you introduced me to it, my sweet."

Trevor walked forward, plucked the book from her hand, and slid it back into the bookshelf, flush with its fellows.

"*Dracula* is one of the most beautiful love stories of all time." His voice was harsh, his breathing quick. "His wife was *murdered* by the treachery of his foul enemies and, rather than exist without her, he chose an immortal life, having faith that their love was so strong, she would be born again to be with him." He leaned in closer. "Even her engagement to another man could not keep her from her *real* love, her *eternal* love with the man who had waited hundreds of years to be with her." Trevor leaned closer and closer with each word.

"I thought..." She swallowed hard. "The immortal love part, is that in the book?" It wasn't. It was created for the 1990's movie version and repeated as canon ever since. All those hours on the internet researching Dracula to please her new boyfriend now fell flat. The vampire in the original *Dracula* was simply a monster. He didn't love, he didn't long for connection. He just killed and fed and controlled.

"What do you know?" Trevor stepped away from her. "You know nothing of vampires, nothing of love."

Ben's face flashed in front of her eyes. Even Nikolai for a second, although a love of a different kind. *I know love. It's just not with you.* She bit her tongue.

"Perhaps not. Perhaps I still need to learn about love." She kept her voice calm, but her jaw was so tense, the words barely scraped by her clenched teeth. "But perhaps we can learn together. Part of love is talking with each other, trying to understand each other."

Trevor eyed her, pacing back and forth between her and the bed like a caged beast.

"Communication can be hard. Here, I'll start." Lauren took a deep breath. "The *hortari* commands. *I feel...*" She put extra emphasis on the *I feel* statement lauded by marriage gurus everywhere. "...that the *hortari* is being used to command me to do things that I would happily do if asked politely." She stepped forward to place a hand on his arm. "I really wish you would stop, it's unkind."

"*Unkind?* I am your sire!" Trevor shouted, stepping away from her. "It is my *right* to shape you, to teach you to be who you are supposed to be!"

"And who am I *supposed* to be?" she asked. *Not good, not good, not good.* Her heart hammered in her chest.

"My love!" He pulled at his hair, his pacing speeding up to an intense prowl back and forth across the room. "You *are* my Felicity, don't you see? Your gracefulness, your voice, your hair. You are her. Born again to be with me!"

Lauren stepped back, found the bookshelf too close, and inched to the side, trying to edge herself closer to the door. "What are you talking about?"

"You are the one! You were born to love me! To obey me! This time you will do as I say!"

"No. We're done, Trevor. I don't know who this Felicity was, or what happened between the two of you, but I'm not her. I'm me. And if you can't see that using the *hortari* to completely control my life is wrong, then we are *really* done." She made a break for the door, sprinting at top speed.

Trevor was faster. "You bitch!" His arm clenched around her midsection, lifting her off the ground. She screamed and kicked.

"Let me down! Stop this!"

"You are my love!" He threw her across the room and she landed hard against the wall, sending a painting of a Romanian castle crashing to the floor in a shower of glass. Lauren bounced off the hard surface, landing on her side amidst glass shards on the carpeting.

"You should *burn* for me." Trevor growled.

Everything hurt. The window had cracked from the force of her hitting the wall, glass imbedded in the palms of her hands. She groaned, pushing herself up and pulling the glass out of her hand. The wound closed immediately, but the pain remained, deep bruises forming where her ribs were cracked, and her leg twisted uncomfortably beneath her.

Lauren glared at him from the floor. "You're a monster."

If he heard, he ignored her, stalking forward until he put two fingers under her chin and dragged her upward until she stood on shaking legs. He leaned close. "You'll learn your lesson. You *will* burn for me. Burn through the night, my love."

The *hortari* took control and Lauren screamed. More pain than she'd ever experienced in her life blazed along her skin. She burned like she was on fire; every part of her skin felt raw and inflamed.

Burn through the night, he'd said. The night still had hours to go. *No!*

Desperation gave her strength. She pushed Trevor away, spinning to leap through the cracked window and plummeted two stories down to the backyard. Glass rained down around her, but the cuts were meaningless compared to the imaginary fire which consumed her. She stumbled across the property, screaming and crying, and dove into the pool.

The water closed around her in comforting coolness, but the burning didn't stop. Her nightgown pooled around her, even the soft lace too much pressure on her raw skin. She tossed the fabric away and sank down to the bottom of the pool. Vampires couldn't drown. The water was quiet.

A splash sounded above her head and she knew she wasn't alone. Filled with an animalistic panic, she kicked off the bottom, wrenched the pool's ladder from its mooring, and spun, searching for Trevor's inevitable attack.

There was no Trevor, only Ben standing in front of her wearing only pajama bottoms with train sets printed on them. His hands rose in front of him in surrender. "Lauren, it's me."

"Ben." She dropped the ladder with a splash, leaping forward until she was in his arms. His touch against her skin didn't hurt, but also didn't decrease the pain. "Trevor's insane!" She pulled him in closer, pushing her bare breasts to his chest, wrapping her legs around his waist.

"Lauren--" His voice was hesitant, a warning that only a few hours ago they'd stepped back from each other rather than betray their loyalties to Trevor.

She cut him off by pressing her lips to his. "Trevor and I are through." He stiffened in surprise and then melted into her, his hands roaming her bare back and resting on her ass, pulling her hips closer as his cock hardened against her inner thighs through the thin fabric of his pants.

"I've wanted this since we met." She tightened her legs around his waist and grabbed his hands from her ass to firmly plant them on her breasts. He groaned and did as she bid, massaging and stroking her erect nipples. She slipped her fingers down to the elastic waistband of his pajamas and pulled them down until she could stroke his cock in the water.

"Oooo, gods. Yes, don't stop." He groaned, his hips thrusting.

"I dumped Trevor, and he's burning me for it." But was he? Her skin wasn't on fire with pain anymore. It tingled with arousal and lust, burning figuratively with *passion*.

Oh hortari, *you clever curse. It's all about the interpretation.* "Ben, I burn for you. I have since we met. Make love to me. I need you." She sighed and nibbled his earlobe, arousal surging in her core. The movements of their bodies made the water lap playfully against her naked skin.

"Lauren, my love, I burn for you too." His tongue surged into her mouth as his hand slipped down between them and stroked down her slit, finding her clit and massaging it in delicate circles. She flexed her hips to give him better access, her hand pumping his cock in time with his movements. His hard body against hers felt perfect, her torso lining up with his so she could lean forward to kiss him as his fingers worked their magic along her clit and then plunged inside her, never stopping their urgent dance along her most sensitive spot.

Distantly, Lauren heard Trevor blasting OneRepublic and Timbaland's "Apologize" like a moping teenager from the top floor, but Trevor didn't matter any more. Ben's breath in her ear made her tingle, everything enhanced. The scent of his skin made her want to lick all of him she could touch. His intense gaze never left her face as he assessed her pleasure and made small adjustments to his caress along her breast, soaring her to higher heights. Her chest heaved as arousal built in waves, the water lapping at her legs up to her breasts pushing her to such intense pleasure she came screaming, biting hard into Ben's shoulder to muffle the sound.

"That's it, my love." His hand moved in calm strokes along her spine as his cock jumped in her hand. "I love seeing joy on your face."

Lauren kissed his sweet mouth, pulling him close and reaching down to slip his cock inside her--he was so thick, he stretched her walls with a glorious soreness, perfect and lush--then flexed her hips to ride him.

He groaned. "Oh gods, that's amazing." He held her close as he carried her to the wall of the pool, pressing her back up against the side so he could have better leverage to thrust into her warmth, his cock pushing deep into her over and over, withdrawing almost all the way to surge back in again.

She held on so tight, she feared her nails were hurting him, but he just grinned with wild abandon and pounded her harder. She loved it, knowing she was making him lose control, that her clever and kind lover was losing his mind fucking her.

Ben pulled her to the shallowest part of the pool and set her down on the gentle incline, changing the angle of her hips so his cock brushed her clit with each slide inside of her. Pleasure built again, even more intense than the first time, her toes curling as she threw her head back, letting her orgasm take her over and over. His cock stiffened, expanding just as he came inside her.

They lay side by side in the water for a long moment, her skin still pulsing with need. *Burn through the night. Oh, lord.*

She looked up at the moon. Still a few hours to go. "Ben...I need..."

"Don't worry. I've got you." He picked her up and carried her into the pool house, both of them dripping water all the way in the door. The lab was too cluttered to carry her, but he took her hand and led her toward the back of his lab. The lab smelled like ocean water and singed paper, but the slight, lingering smell of pizza made her smile. She stroked Ben's bare back, loving the closeness of him. She trusted him more than anyone she'd ever known. He made her feel safe, loved, just as she loved him.

He kicked aside a carpet and opened up a hidden door in the floor. He flicked on a light next to the door and led the way down a short ladder into his bedroom. It was exactly what she would expect of Ben: utilitarian, with a double bed that had clearly never been made, but smelled clean. A small chest of clothes and a poster of the Periodic Table were the only decorations.

"I'm sorry. It's not exactly luxurious. If you...um...stick around, I can definitely jazz up the place a bit. One of my sireling sisters is a designer and she can--"

Lauren stopped his babbling with a swift kiss. "It's great," she said. "I'm with you. I don't care what the room looks like."

He grinned his beautiful grin and swooped in for a longer kiss, his mouth hot and needy against hers. She pushed them both toward the bed, the two tumbling back onto the unmade covers. Their legs tangled together, their hands trying to touch everything at once. Ben's lips found her neck, kissing a trail down past her breasts and her stomach to settle with his mouth latched firmly to her clit. Lauren cried out, her hands automatically reaching down to curl around his hair and keep him firmly planted there as he licked and kissed her core.

"You taste so good." He licked at her. "I want to always taste my cum on you," he muttered into her pussy.

She arched her back, pressing her flesh closer to his tongue. "Oooo, don't stop. Don't you dare stop."

"Darling, I'm going to eat you out until the sun rises."

She didn't think it was possible to cum so many times. After the fifth, she lost count. An hour later, he recovered enough to fuck her again and she rode him for as long as they could stand, switching positions so he could pound her from behind, and she refused to let him cum again until he was inside her mouth, his salty cum dribbling down her lips and she swallowed deep. She felt addicted to his touch, kissing and stroking everything she could reach. Even after the sun rose and the incessant burning of the *hortari* died away, she couldn't stop kissing him. It was mid-morning before she collapsed into sleep, curled up against Ben's side, his hand even in sleep curled around her breast.

Time was shaky at best in Ben's basement, but she guessed it was at least afternoon, from the way her stomach gurgled, when she woke up. She rolled to her side to see Ben was already awake, looking down at her with an expression of wonder.

"I keep thinking I'll blink and realize I'm dreaming," he said.

"I'm not going to be able to stay here," she said. "Trevor's still my sire, and he won't just let me go."

Ben nodded, his fingers caressing back and forth along her hip in tiny circles. Lauren smiled. Ben couldn't stop moving, even when still in bed. "I know. There are safe places for you to go. My sire, Christopher, has been trying to track down instances of *hortari* abuse, bring the abusers to justice. I can get you to the castle if that's where you want to go."

Lauren laughed, since the alternative was to cry. *There's been a way out all along?* She could have left after that disaster of an opera date. She could have left after the first time his command locked her into doing his will. Sure, he had commanded she couldn't leave the house without supervision, but she could have found a way around it. She *had* found a way around it to go to AUDREY'S with Ben.

"Come with me." She grabbed his hand, held it to her chest cradled between her breasts. "Trevor is a monster. He'll use you just as surely as he used me. Be with me." She'd survived her parents' degradation. She'd survived Trevor's violence. She'd survived her flesh feeling like it was on fire. She had proven she could survive anything on her own. But she didn't *want* to do it alone.

She looked deep into Ben's beautiful eyes. "I love you, Benjamin Dal."

His hands cupped her face. "And I love you, Lauren Vaughan, with everything I am. Wherever you want to go, whatever you want to do, I will follow."

The rest of the day passed in a blur of endearments, remembered moments together eating pizza and chatting about when each realized that they loved the other. Ben said it was the first time she'd pressed bacon pizza into his hand; Lauren admitted she hadn't realized her feelings were love until AUDREY'S. They made love again until Lauren chased them both into the shower to clean up, where they made love again, which meant getting cleaned up again.

Ben slid open the trap door to his lab as the sun slipped over the horizon, glancing about to confirm that Trevor wasn't about. From the sound of the break-up playlist still blasting from the top floor, he hadn't even noticed the noises they were making in the pool the night before.

Not my problem anymore.

She'd borrowed a set of pants and a shirt from Ben's closet, lashing it across her lean body with a belt. The clothes were hopelessly oversized and made her look fat, but she didn't care.

They were getting out of here. Together, they crept out of the pool house, sticking to the shadows along the fence. Ben pulled out a device and pointed it at his home. It shimmered for a second before shrinking down to the size of a quarter.

Lauren stared. She'd been *inside* that house. She'd *slept* in that house. She glanced at the device in Ben's hand. *Fucking hell.* Only the pneumatic tube which led from the side of the pool house into the mansion remained, a reaching hand to nowhere. Ben jogged over to pick up the button-sized home and pop it into a plastic bag he pulled from his pocket.

"You have no idea how many times I've dropped this and flooded my house." He winked at her and tapped at the bag. "This helps."

Lauren giggled and rolled her eyes. "Let's just get out of here."

BRANCHES CRUNCHED under Ben's boots as they ran along the forest trail, super vampiric speed making short work of their progress along the back of Trevor's estate. Ben resisted the urge to laugh, to jump for joy.

Lauren turned towards Ben and smiled, her face lighting up the night more brightly than the full moon. They had come to a point where they didn't need to speak words to be understood. *I love you*, her face beamed at him. *I love you back*, Ben indicated with a squeeze of her hand. Everything was perfect. Almost.

They just had to get away before Trevor realized they weren't coming back. Lauren didn't need to face whatever that jerk tossed her way if they encountered him.

Following a different path than they'd taken to get out when they went to AUDREY'S in case Trevor was on the lookout for them, they hurried through the trees to get to the less-security-covered back door of the garage.

Lauren slowed their run to a stroll, guiding Ben to match her pace. "I think the well...everything took it out of me." She panted. "Let's just walk." Lauren wrapped her arm around Ben's back and leaned into him as they strolled along.

"This is nice." Ben sighed. "I've been living in that pool house for so long, only leaving when Christopher summoned me for something. I was so focused on my work, I never took the time to explore the grounds. I almost missed seeing how much beauty there is in the world." He never took his eyes off of Lauren.

Lauren blushed, looking down. "I wouldn't have pegged Trevor for the gardening type."

She was changing the subject and it made Ben sad. Could she really not accept how much he cared for her? *It's a good thing I have all the time in the world to convince her.*

Lauren knelt down next to a wide patch of yellow flowers with purple spots. "Can you picture him, rooting in the dirt with a trowel and a big, floppy hat?" She leaned in to give one of the flowers a sniff.

"No!" Ben jumped forward and lifted Lauren into his arms.

He'd been so focused on Lauren's beautiful face, he hadn't taken a good look at the flowers. Horror crept up Ben's spine as he stared down at the flowers he'd only ever seen once before.

"Keep back from those. They're harmful to our kind."

"Really?" Lauren took a step back, her eyes narrowed as she studied the flowers at her feet. "I've never heard of anything like that. Beheading and fire, those both make sense for taking down us vamps. But flower power?"

"These are kkot. They're incredibly rare. They take a certain amount of *effort* to grow." He swallowed down rising bile. "They won't kill you, but contact with a kkot puts vampires in a deep sleep. Ingesting, touching, or even smelling the flower can knock one of us out cold."

She studied his face, her eyebrows puckered in worry.

"There's more to this, isn't there? Why would Trevor grow a flower that could harm him?"

Ben shook his head, stepping back further from the flowers, holding Lauren's hand tight. *There are so many. So very many.*

Lauren squeezed Ben's hand. "Tell me." She nodded firmly. "I want to know."

"I've only seen this once before: my uncle, Rhys, had a mass grave of all of his enemies." Ben swallowed hard and turned to Lauren. "Kkot only grows in the soil where *a lot* of vampires have been buried together." The words came slowly as the full implication of what Trevor had done, of what his nephew had become while Ben wasn't paying attention, chilled him to his core. "These are trophies. The flowers. For kkot clusters like this to grow, he has to be dumping the bodies all together, so the flowers would remind him of what he did."

I should have noticed a long time ago. All those girlfriends. *I should have stopped him. I should have told Danny, told Christopher, told anyone.* "Underneath our feet lay dozens of dead vampires."

Lauren gasped, her hand going to her throat and she swallowed loud. "Oh, gods." She paced back and forth in a small circle behind Ben. "I *knew* Trevor could be a sadistic asshole, but this is insane. Murder?" She turned to Ben.

Ben wished he could say something comforting, tell her that it was all some silly misunderstanding and they weren't presently standing over a mass grave. He wanted to pull her into his arms and assure her that everything was going to be okay.

I've been living alongside a serial killer, collaborating in business with a serial killer. Ben closed his eyes, then forced himself to open them and really look at the flowers. He wasn't responsible for Trevor becoming a monster, but he was responsible for ignoring his doubts.

"I can't let Trevor keep doing this to people. Gods, you could have been next..." The mere thought of Trevor harming Lauren, that she might have soon disappeared under the cold earth, was like taking a punch to the gut. Ben staggered backwards.

"*We* have to stop him." Lauren's fists clenched tight. "He can't just use women up and dispose of them like broken dolls."

Ben nodded. "I have to stop him. I'm older, and therefore stronger, than he is. I'll contact his sire, Danny, and the king, but we can't risk Trevor realizing we're both gone and escaping. I need to go back." He took Lauren's hand in his own. "You're newly-turned, and still under his command. You should walk away, hide out someplace, and wait for me to find you. If I take Trevor down, nothing will get in our way. We can be together, and we can be safe."

He knew Lauren's answer before she spoke the words. She was strong in so many ways. She wasn't going to take a back seat.

"Don't be stupid." She pulled Ben close for a deep kiss, her tongue running a quick, delicious lap around his mouth. "I'm coming with you. We're going to take this bastard down together."

Ben held Lauren close. His eyes swept over the graves, the

kkot flowers the only markers of the lives that had been extinguished. "I have an idea."

LAUREN'S FEET softly padded through the grass as she made a quick loop around the perimeter of the house, peering into each window. She found Trevor's shadow prowling around the top floor of his bedroom. Just seeing his outline made her feet still like a deer caught in the fatal head beams of a truck.

We have to stop him. Her words to Ben got her moving again. She crept around to the entrance of the east wing, her palms sweating before she even slipped inside.

Trevor's house had always been creepy, but knowing that it was the home of a serial killer made the oppressive darkness of the place even more skin-crawling. The lines of stone arches embedded in the ceiling reminded her of rib caves, and the high, dark windows were like too many eyes peering down at her.

The pneumatic tube ran into the east wing, half of which was taken up by a gym. She wondered if the exercise area had come with the house, since it wasn't like anyone living here actually needed to work out. When he was first showing her around, Trevor had even discouraged her from using any of the equipment. At the time, she'd thought he was just explaining another advantage of being a vampire, but could there have been more to it than that? *Was he ensuring I'd stay weaker, unable to fight back?*

Lauren pushed the thought down. She couldn't think about how she had *sex* with a serial killer. Those memories of pleasure on the restaurant floor promising a future of security were as tainted as kkot-planted soil. Bile rose and she choked it down before the smell told Trevor where she was.

Think of Ben, think of goodness, think about how we're going to get the rat bastard.

She almost tripped over Trevor's SCUBA tanks lining the mirrored wall of the gym. They'd worn those SCUBA tanks when on a spectacular trip to Sharm el Sheikh outside Cairo, back when he'd been pretending to be human and that he actually needed to breathe under water.

How couldn't I see he was such a monster? There had to have been signs. Long talks about art, history, music, and where they were going to go next for six months. Trevor would do most of the talking and Lauren would smile and nod, every few minutes asking a question to let Trevor keep talking about his interests. But never about himself. They'd never talked about past relationships, and she'd avoided bringing it up for fear she'd let slip about her previous marriage over too many glasses of wine.

I wanted him to be my savior, so I ignored the warning signs.

She rubbed between her eyes, forcing her gaze away from the tanks and their reminder of how deeply--in her desperation to find someone to provide for her--she'd failed herself.

Lauren found the lever for the pneumatic tube exactly where Ben said it was going to be: a red handle hidden behind a box of what looked like costumes from a Shakespeare play. She triumphantly flipped a switch on the panel from Auto to Manual. The clock in the east wing's tower chimed it was eight and Lauren slipped on her gas mask before the chimes stopped. A sound of hissing air came from the long tube. She smiled.

Back in the re-sized pool house, Ben had ground up the kkot flowers they'd spent the last few hours carefully harvesting, and he'd used one of his gadgets to convert their petals into a gas. He had the expertise to pump the gas through the pneumatic tube into the house, but someone on the other side had to open up the hatch and ensure that the gas made it all the way in to knock out Trevor.

By Ben's calculations, the gas would hit Trevor's room quickly, filling it in under thirty seconds and then moving out to the rest of house. Kkot was brutal: one whiff and he'd be unconscious for hours. Lauren smiled grimly at the thought. It would be a small revenge for those who were gone, but Lauren liked the thought that the flowers which marked Trevor's victims would be part of what took him down.

After she engaged the pneumatic tube, the plan was for Lauren to get out as quickly as possible. Once Ben filled the house with gas, he'd stop the pump, and come collect Trevor for transport to the castle for judgment.

Lauren made it all the way to the back door before she stopped, her hand shying away from the door knob. She looked back at the stairs, memories haunting her of her feet being commanded to cross that room, of standing at Trevor's mercy.

She *needed* to see Trevor unconscious. Before Ben came in and took control of the situation, she wanted to see Trevor helpless at her feet, done in by their plan.

Before she lost her nerve, she ran up the stairs to Trevor's room, scanning the ground for any sign of his motionless body. He wasn't in his bedroom, or the library, or her room, or any of the bathrooms. She even pulled back the shower curtains, her heart hammering in her chest, old horror movie instincts kicking in as she braced for what might be behind.

But nothing. Every room was empty.

Did he escape? If he'd slipped out onto the grounds, then Ben might be in trouble. She ran as fast as she could, doing one last sweep of all the rooms to make sure. The gas had to have permeated every room of the house by now--Ben had rigged the pneumatic tube to connect with the vents once it got inside for maximum coverage.

Lauren made it halfway through the last storage room before she realized that something was wrong. She backtracked, chasing a feeling that she was missing something crucial. She stopped short at the gym, scanning the rows of SCUBA gear until she counted.

One was missing, an outline of dust on the floor marking where it had sat until recently.

Oh shit.

A flash of movement in the corner of her eye was the only warning she got. Lauren dropped to the ground ducking under the wild swing of a SCUBA tank.

Trevor swung fast at her face and she rolled out of the way, jumping to her feet as the clash of metal against hardwood shook the floor. She dove over the steps of a stair climber and grabbed four kettlebells from the rack by the wall. Adrenaline surged.

Trevor's face contorted in a grimace and memories of being humiliated at the opera, of getting hurtled into his bedroom wall, feeling like she was burning to death plucked at the corner of her mind, fueling her rage. The weights felt as light as pebbles to her vampire strength and she flung them as fast as she could at Trevor's oncoming form. One hit his shoulder, the other his chest, but two missed, flying harmlessly over his shoulder to embed in the opposite wall.

He howled and ran toward her. She ducked and rolled under his outstretched hands, punching him hard in the groin as she slid beneath him. He doubled over, but recovered quickly, jumping away from her attempts to pull off the gas mask which protected him from the kkot.

Inside his SCUBA gear, Trevor's mouth moved in what Lauren guessed from the confident sneer on his face were commands.

Lauren laughed, pointing to her earplugs, firmly in place. "I can't hear you, you asshole!"

His second of shock was all she needed. Lauren leapt forward and yanked away Trevor's face mask. He grabbed his nose with one hand, closing his mouth. His triumphant glare communicated what he couldn't dare open his mouth to voice: *vampires don't need to breathe, you fool.*

Lauren picked up the SCUBA tank and swung with all of her might. It connected with Trevor's skull with a clang that reverberated through the room and shook the mirrors on the wall. Trevor gasped in shock at the blow, taking in a deep breath of kkot. He fell over to the ground, and lay still. Lauren stood over him.

She almost kicked him in the face, but stopped herself. *I'm better than him.* She used chains pulled from the exercise equipment to hogtie his hands and feet together behind his back. With a happy sigh, she pulled out her earplugs.

Ben ran through the door a second later, his face also covered with a gas mask.

"I heard the sounds of banging. Are you all right?" he asked, running forward to pull her into his arms and study Trevor's slow breathing.

"I'm more than all right." Lauren smiled wide, showing every tooth. "I won."

"GUILTY ON ALL COUNTS!" The judge's voice echoed through the royal courthouse; it was quickly overcome by cheers.

Ben pulled Lauren into his arms and spun her in a tight circle. She laughed and held tightly onto him.

"Trevor will never be able to hurt you or anyone else ever again." Ben brought her back to the ground and held her close.

"Damn straight," Lauren joked, wrapping her arms around Ben's neck and pulling him in for a long, lingering kiss. Her hair, which she had down and wild, tickled his nose, and her overjoyed smile warmed him to his toes.

"Hey, no making out in the court!" A voice interrupted them.

Ben turned to see Danny Dal, hand-in-hand with his fiancé Robin, striding towards Ben and Lauren down the hallway.

"It's good to see you." Danny shook Ben's hand. "I can't believe things with Trevor got so out of hand." He sighed. "I knew he had some weird ideas about Dracula and all, but this..." He pointed at the evidence still tacked up on a bulletin board: the faces of the fifty six women Trevor had killed over the centuries.

Trevor had admitted everything during the trial. Ben suspected the egomaniacal pipsqueak had been longing to talk about his "dark romance" as he called it, for a long time. Back when he was still human, Trevor had a crush on a woman named Felicity. She was disgusted by him, so Trevor begged Danny to turn him, in hopes that Felicity would find Trevor more appealing as a 'creature of the night'. When that didn't work, Trevor spent centuries turning women who looked like Felicity, controlling them to fulfill the delusional fantasies he'd envisioned for his life with his "true love". Whenever one of his sirelings deviated from the script in his head, Trevor killed her and turned another.

"I'm beyond grateful that you were able to bring him to justice," Danny said, his expression grave. "I should have never turned him, or at least I should have kept a better eye on him."

"I didn't stop him alone." Ben wrapped his arm around Lauren's waist. "This is Lauren, the *real* brains behind our operation." He rested his index finger on his chin. "And the brawn, too, now that I think about it."

Robin nudged Danny with her elbow, her laugh bringing a smile to Danny's dour face. "I believe it. It's such hard work keeping these dashing men in line, isn't it?"

"Non-stop toil, really." Lauren's tone was somber, but she was grinning wildly.

"So what's next for you two?" Danny asked. "Trevor's mansion is in my name. It's yours if you want it. You can move out of the pool house and live large for a change."

"We're sticking with the pool house," Lauren said.

Ben pulled a clear plastic bag out of his pocket and held it at eye level. "We'll just be taking it with us." The miniaturized pool house was inside, but now closer to the size of a baseball than a button. He'd added a few new rooms to his home while it was still miniaturized--much easier and cost-effective to do it that way--and Lauren had been completely enchanted by what he'd built for her.

"That'll explain the outfit, then." Danny failed to stifle a laugh.

"What?" Ben looked down at his head-to-toe khaki ensemble. He'd bought what he had been assured by centuries of reading fiction was the exact correct thing to wear. The wide-brimmed hat was a bit large for his head, and the binoculars he had tucked into one of the overly-large pockets weighed him down a bit, but he'd never been more excited.

"I think he looks adorable." Lauren squeezed his arm. "We're going on a world tour, starting with a safari. Ben's desalinator has helped so many people in so many countries, I think it's only fair that he gets to see how much good he's done in person. And I'm looking forward to roaming free for a change. With our house in a bag, we can go anywhere we want at any time."

Ben's chest swelled with pride. Once his desalination machine was finished, Lauren had helped him load up the specs online so people all over the globe could build their own. Clean drinking water was now easily available in places where it was once seen as a luxury.

Lauren twined her fingers through Ben's and whispered in his ear. "I love you, you know."

"I love you, too." Ben pulled her close. He had an idea for proposing once they reached Kenya, but he wasn't sure he'd be able to wait that long.

They walked out of the courtroom, away from Trevor and the van taking him to the hole in the ground he was going to live in for the foreseeable future. The only thing that mattered was Lauren and Ben moving forward together.

"Let's go dancing" Ben said.

Lauren kissed him. "With you? Always."

Our vampire adventures conclude in the action-packed final installment of the *Royal Blood* series, *The Vampire's Choice*.

Dear Reader,

We hoped you enjoyed **The Vampire's Escape.** We really love this world and creating more places and people to inhabit it. Many readers wrote asking; "What's up with Lola?" Well, stay tuned for more of Lola's mysterious meddling because the adventures at AUDREY'S (and the paranormal romantic interludes) aren't over.

When we first published this series, we got a lot of emails from fans thanking us for these books. Some liked certain series and sets of characters more than others. As authors, we love feedback. Your appreciation for this world is the reason why we keep writing books in this world.

Reviews are increasingly tough to come by these days. You, the reader, have the power now to make or break a book. So, tell us what you like, what you loved, even what you hated. We'd love to hear from you.

Thank you so much for reading **The Vampire's Escape** and for spending time with our wacky brains.

Have fun, everybody

Annie & Jess ("AJ") Tipton

MEET AJ TIPTON

AJ Tipton is the pseudonym of a writing team: Annie and Jess (Get it? "AJ." You get it). Corporate drones by day, we spend our evenings writing fantasies to astound, arouse, and amuse. Located in Brooklyn, we are total dorks and love it.

Want more stories of the bizarre and wondrous? Sign up for the new publications subscription list and you'll be the first to know when new books become available. There might also be other surprises along the way. Or just contact us directly at a.j.tipton.author@gmail.com

Our ideas for future books--everything from sex robots to ghost brothels--will keep us busy for many years to come, so follow along for the fun and let us know what series you like best. We love to hear from readers.

ajtiptonauthor.wordpress.com
ajtiptonauthor@gmail.com

Made in United States
Orlando, FL
03 October 2024

52334284R00055